W9-CFB-583

ROUGH JUSTICE

Center Point
Large Print

Also by Lauran Paine and available from
Center Point Large Print:

Beyond Fort Mims
Ute Peak Country
Way of the Outlaw
The Plains of Laramie
Guns in Wyoming
Man from Durango
Prairie Empire
Sheriff of Hangtown

ROUGH JUSTICE

A Western Story

LAURAN PAINE

CENTER POINT LARGE PRINT
THORNDIKE, MAINE

This Circle Ⓥ Western is published by
Center Point Large Print in 2014 in co-operation with
Golden West Literary Agency.

First Edition
June, 2014

The text of this Large Print edition is unabridged.
In other aspects, this book may vary
from the original edition.
Printed in the United States of America
on permanent paper.
Set in 16-point Times New Roman type.

ISBN: 978-1-62899-113-0

Library of Congress Cataloging-in-Publication Data

Paine, Lauran.
  Rough justice : a western story / Lauran Paine. — First edition.
  pages ; cm
  Summary: "Sheriff Doyle Bannion tries to keep the peace in Perdition
Wells, Texas, when the four King brothers ride in bent on avenging their
father's death"— Provided by publisher.
  ISBN 978-1-62899-113-0 (library binding : alk. paper)
  1. Large type books. I. Title.
  PS3566.A34R68 2014
  813′.54—dc23
                                                            2014006660

ROUGH JUSTICE

Chapter One

They came in the night with a desert wind at their backs, four swift riders with sheepskin windbreakers turned up at the throat and four black guns lashed low to their legs. They left their animals at the livery barn and braced the wintertime blow as far as the sheriff's office. They pushed inside with their solid tread and stood silently, stood stalwartly, filling that small office, gazing at Sheriff Doyle Bannion with wind whistling in from the storm-lashed roadway.

Remaining seated, Bannion returned the stare of these large men, waiting for them to speak, to close the door, to pass over to his chairs along the wall and sit. They did none of these things. They stood looking down while the lamp guttered, while shadows sprang to life upon the far adobe wall, their strong, bony faces, somehow alike, fixed downward in an unpleasant way.

In this groaning night beyond, the Santa Ana wind, up out of Mexico, beat with powerful force upon the town making shakes slap, and siding creak, and windows rattle. There was cutting dust in that wind, the kind that, when breathed deeply, brought blood in a man's cough. It was the Santa Ana time of year, neither spring nor winter. The desert churned, it rose up and flung away, it covered tracks and sand-blasted buildings, and drove livestock headlong ahead of it in a blind seeking for shelter.

Bannion got up and closed the door. He closed it hard and went back to his desk. He said: "All right . . . you've made your point. Now what the hell do you want in Perdition Wells?"

The eldest of those four men spoke without moving. "I guess you could say we want justice. But I reckon a place called Perdition would be a poor place to get it."

Doyle Bannion eased back. He had broken the spell these big men cast, and when that oldest one had answered, the break was permanent. "The name," said Bannion, "was put on this town because there's a hot water spring east of here." He looked steadily up at that big man, guessed him to be in his late twenties or early thirties, and said: "I've heard all the jokes there are about Perdition Wells and don't any of them seem very funny to me any more. The Mexicans named this place, but they don't own Texas any more so maybe someday someone'll get around to changing the name. I hope so. Now . . . what can I do for you?"

"You can give us the name of a murderer," said the spokesman of those four night riders.

"First you'll have to tell me who got murdered. Then if I can, I'll oblige you."

The youngest of those big men, in his late teens with a smooth face and a clear eye, said: "The name was King. Alpheus King."

Doyle Bannion let out his breath in a long, quiet way and for an interval of full silence said nothing. He gauged those four big men, assessed the depths of their temper, the degrees of their leashed violence, and felt lead settle in his belly, for there was no way not to see that these men were also named King.

"Listen to me," he told them. "First I'll explain how that happened." They did not interrupt, or even move for that matter, but the solid weight of their combined judgments was filling Bannion's office with a blind and uncompromising stubbornness. "Old Al was swamper at the Union Eagle Saloon. There was an argument. When the smoke cleared, Al was down dead with a bullet through the heart."

"No warning?" asked Hank King, next oldest after Ray.

Bannion said: "Let me ask you boys something. How were you related to the old man?"

"His sons," answered Hank.

Bannion's gaze clouded. "I see. Well, maybe you hadn't seen him for a long time."

"What's that got to do with it?"

"He was warned, boys. There were some calls, they tell me, but Al was pretty deaf. He went right on sweeping. If it's any satisfaction, and I reckon

9

it wouldn't be if he'd been my paw, old Al never knew what hit him."

"We're obliged," murmured Ray King, the eldest. "You've been right helpful, Sheriff. Now the name."

Bannion saw no change in those four expressions and felt no change in the atmosphere. "Another question," he said. "Why was he here in Perdition Wells, if he had sons and a home?"

"He had no home, Sheriff," said Austin King, the youngest. "How good's your memory?"

"It's good enough. Why?"

"You recollect King's Raiders?"

Doyle Bannion's gaze brightened slightly. "King's Confederate Raiders?"

"That's right."

"Who doesn't remember," Bannion said quietly. "The only authorized Confederate guerilla band that was not given amnesty after the war." Bannion looked from one of them to the others. "Was he *that* King?"

The big men nodded and Bannion eased back in his chair, remembering how it had been many years before when the Federal Union and the embattled South were fighting it out toe-to-toe in the bloody Shenandoah, on the peninsula, and along the turgid Río Grande. King's Confederate Raiders had been a knout and a scourge to the Yankees. They rarely struck twice in the same place, they came swirling out of the dawn without warning, they were pursued, and they were dreaded. But they had never been apprehended, and after Appomattox they had simply dissolved, still undefeated.

For ten years, long after others had been given total amnesty by a victorious Federal Union, secret service operatives, manhunters, and federal lawyers had pushed an intense search for the officers of King's Raiders. None had ever been captured, and now, so many decades later, the aura of mystery and romance, of gallantry, had cloaked this dim memory with a sympathetic mantle, particularly among Texans, for it had been known that Colonel King's officers had all come from the Lone Star state.

"That King," said Doyle Bannion again, beginning to understand the scope of this dilemma. "He was a saloon swamper."

"He never quit running, Sheriff. He never quit hiding. He was an old man. They wouldn't let him go his last years in peace. There are a dozen orders for arrest out for him right now. But you'd know that, wouldn't you?"

Bannion nodded. "I've got some posters about him, yes. But I don't believe there are ten lawmen in all Texas who would have arrested him, boys."

"It's those ten he's been running from."

Bannion looked at his hands. "It's hard to believe. Colonel Al King . . . swamper in the Union Eagle Saloon here in Perdition Wells."

11

Nostalgic bitterness touched down through Bannion. "A real hero in his time, a great Confederate and a legendary guerrilla raider."

The eldest King loosened a little in his stance. He regarded Doyle Bannion without hardness. "That's how it goes when a man lives beyond his usefulness. Every now and then someone would recognize him and send one of us word. We'd go at once where he was. We'd take him money and news of his kinfolk. Some years back our mother . . . his wife . . . got down bedfast . . . she'd tell us things to say to him. We'd carry the message back and forth. Once, he wanted to go back, but there were Secret Service men watching and he couldn't. She died that winter. After that he kept getting harder and harder to find."

Bannion got up, crossed to a little stove, poked up a fire, and jiggled the coffee pot there, hefted it, then said: "There's enough." He pointed to a row of tin cups dangling from nails beneath a wooden shelf. "Help yourselves."

Ray King, the eldest, said: "No thanks Sheriff. All we want here is a name."

Bannion poured himself a cupful very slowly and watched that black liquid fill his cup in its oily way. He then returned to his chair and sat down without looking up at those four big men.

How do you say it? the sheriff wondered. *Let the old devil go. Let him get plumb away from this earth. Don't hold him here with more killings.*

Sure he was your paw, but he's sick to death. He just wants to be left alone in peaceful solitude, to lie in hushed darkness and forget. If you kill the man who shot him, you'll be bringing the old man back to torment, to suffering. You'll be chaining him to this damned life he was thoroughly weary of. He won't be able to get away because the killing won't stop when you get the fool who accidentally killed him. There will be a whole row of killings, and, because he'll be the cause, he'll have to stay here and suffer his anguish and his damnation. How do you say that to the Texas sons of a murdered man? You don't. Bannion knew you didn't because he was a Texan, too.

"The name, Sheriff."

The coffee was like acid. Bannion pushed it away, telling himself that he had to try. Even though he could see in their unwavering eyes, in the hard-set jut of their jaws that he could not win, still he had to try. He owed this to his badge, his oath, more than anything else he owed it to himself, because, if the King boys did not know what lay ahead, Bannion knew, and he therefore had to warn them against it.

"I know how it is with you fellers. I've seen this before, except that there's a difference here. A unique difference. Boys, your paw wants it all to end right here. The bullet that killed him was fired into his heart by accident. But I am plumb certain it was a relief to him.

13

"I knew him right well. Even though I thought he was just another old-timer without a dime or kin, we were friends. I felt the sadness in him, but, hell, all lonely old men got sadness in them after life has passed them by. I know now what that sadness was. I know as well as I'm sitting here, he wants it all to end right now. No more killings, no more running and hiding." Bannion sat forward, clasped his hands, and looked at them.

"You know that war is like throwing a stone into a still pool. The ripples spread and spread and keep on spreading. Each ripple is the wake of something unfinished, something left over after the last bugle's been blown, and men can either turn away and let those ripples die out, or they can keep those ripples widening, running on and touching lives forty years later." Bannion looked up at them—at Ray the eldest, at Hank next eldest, at Al—named for his paw—third eldest, and finally at Austin, the youngest. "That's what you boys are doing now. You're keeping one of those ripples spreading. Don't do it. The colonel wouldn't want you to, believe me about that."

Bannion stopped speaking. Silence settled filling the room. It came gently, layers and layers of it, until there was no place for any more.

Then young Austin spoke into it. "The name, Sheriff."

"No, not from me."

"A friend, Sheriff?"

"Not a friend, an acquaintance is all." Bannion looked up. There was no change in any of those faces. No change at all. Austin was young and proud and fiery. Next to him was Al. There was something here—something felt but indefinably elusive. Something a little frightening.

Then there was Hank. He and Ray seemed settled in their maturity. Hard men and deadly men, but not unfair men. The trouble with Ray and Hank was, like their brothers, they had come of age believing in the gun and what it insured them. A man killed to defend himself and the things he loved or believed in. He killed to make his Texas plains and hills and towns safe places for other Texans who shared his convictions. And he killed for vengeance, to set right some particular wrong done him or his.

It was a very old law and it was held to be the best justice on earth, not only by Texans, but especially by them. An eye for an eye and a tooth for a tooth.

"We'll find the name, Sheriff."

"Yes," conceded Doyle Bannion, rising. "You'll find it. I can't prevent that. But you'll find a lot more, too, boys. A hell of a lot more, because that name will only be the beginning."

Bannion passed around them to the door and opened it. That screaming wind got inside to make the lamp gutter and smoke darkly.

"Good night, boys."

"Good night, Sheriff."

They went out into the raw night and stood close to the building, considering Perdition Wells—its broad roadway, its orange-lighted saloons and variety houses, and its few cursing pedestrians who went along bracing either into the wind or against it.

Looking steadily up where a full hitch rack and the noise and gaiety of a crowded saloon emanated, Al said: "I need a drink."

The others followed out Al's line of vision, saw the quivering sign that said in bold black letters **Union Eagle Saloon**, and started forward with their brother, four abreast across the scourged roadway, up onto another plank walk and down it all the way to that lighted, noisy place. Then they headed inside where tobacco smoke lay thick as fog and people made a noise as vibrant as the lashing outside wind.

Chapter Two

Doyle Bannion shrugged into his windbreaker, pulled his hat on hard, and went along to the livery barn. He got his horse and rode north, then east, with sharp particles of razor-like dust grating in the folds of his neck and around his flattened lips.

He rode with a kind of helplessness weighing down his spirit, and two hours later when he swung out and down before a big wood house, white-painted and ghostly in the gusty night, Doyle Bannion could definitely feel the solid futility of what he was about to do. He tied his horse fast to a stud post and stepped up onto the porch planking. It felt as though he were a chip being blown first one way and then another way by a wind of circumstance and ritual stronger than he, or any other man, could ever hope to be.

There were lights showing from a long adobe house across this big yard. Farther out stood an immense log barn and its connecting spidery network of pole corrals. An air of prosperity, of power, of durability and lasting substance lay over this big ranch that no Santa Ana wind could even touch. It was the power that lingered in Doyle's thoughts. The power brought by wealth.

The power that eroded men's spirits and made them swell with arrogance.

He knocked on the door.

Borne fitfully by that soughing wind was music from the adobe bunkhouse—the lift and ebb of a man's pleasant voice. There was also a soft scent of white oak burning in a stove somewhere, mingled with the more permanent scent of cattle.

The door opened. A big man stood there near to filling the opening. He was a handsome, broad man with gray over his temples and a confident, near smile down around his lips. He had a high-bridge nose and bold glance. "Sheriff," he said, sounding surprised, sounding confident, and not in the least apprehensive. "Come in out of the cold."

Bannion crossed the threshold and halted there. Beyond, past a mahogany partition, burned a warming fire. A woman sat with her back to Bannion, and near her a girl with hair the color of new gold and flesh as good to look upon as fresh-churned butter. Bannion knew them both.

"Come into the parlor," the handsome man said, closing the door and smiling his solid smile.

"No. What I got to say I'd best say right here," responded Doyle Bannion, looking solemn and wind-whipped. "Mister Rockland, that old man who was accidentally killed when Dale McAfee and that cowboy from Clell Durham's outfit shot it out at the Union Eagle couple months ago was Colonel Alpheus King."

Bannion kept a steady look at Rockland's face, waiting for understanding to come.

Rockland stood a moment returning this regard, then he rolled his brows together in a puzzled way, saying: "No . . . you don't mean . . . ? Hell, man, you couldn't possibly mean *the* Colonel King from back during the war . . . the Colonel King of King's Confederate Raiders."

"Yes, sir, that's exactly who I mean."

John Rockland stared at Bannion. His lips faintly lifted at their outer corners. His eyes showed a gradual shading of quiet and amused irony. "I'll be damned," he breathed. "I thought that old devil had passed on years ago. You used to hear all sorts of stories. . . . He was seen down in Mexico. He was living in the wilds of upper Canada with Indians. He was actually the governor out in California in disguise." Rockland made his easy, assured smile at Bannion. "Are you sure?"

Before Bannion could answer, Rockland raised a hand, roughly tapped Bannion's chest, and chuckled. "No," he scoffed. "Those old tramps just say things like that. No, Bannion. It's just another Colonel King legend."

"Mister Rockland, this is no made-up story."

Bannion's dead earnestness was grave enough to brush past Rockland's faint amusement. Quietly the larger man began to lose his appearance of scorn, of sardonic amusement. He said: "Go on, Doyle. What else is on your mind?"

"Colonel King's four sons rode into Perdition Wells tonight, Mister Rockland. They want the name of the man who killed their father."

"Oh?" Rockland said, his tone changing, becoming soft and dangerous. "And what do these four men propose to do?"

"Kill Dale McAfee."

Rockland's bold gaze got steady, brittle, and unwaveringly iron-like. It remained upon Sheriff Bannion.

"You'd better run them out of town, Bannion. Better yet . . . you'd better tell them Dale McAfee works for me, and that I take care of my own." Rockland paused, then said in a condescending way: "Tell them it was an accident . . . that the old fool got behind Clell Durham's rider and that the same bullet that killed Durham's cowboy also killed their father. It's too bad, but that's the way it happened. A pure accident and no one is to blame."

"Mister Rockland, I already told them that."

Bannion's stubborn persistence in the face of Rockland's attempt at dismissing this thing appeared to annoy the cowman.

He said: "Bannion, you enforce the law. Get those men out of Perdition Wells." Then Rockland said exactly what Bannion knew he was going to say. "If you don't, I will. I'm sorry about the old man, but it was an absolute accident, and I don't care if he was old Jeff Davis or Robert E. Lee, he's dead and that's got to be the end of it." Rockland waited a moment, then brought up his easy smile again. "Come, have some coffee with us," he said.

Bannion turned, opened the door, and started back through it and out into the wild night. "No thanks, Mister Rockland. If I were you I wouldn't try to run those men out of town, either."

"No?"

"No, sir. Ride in tomorrow and take a good long look at them before you try it."

Bannion closed the door very softly, resettled his hat on his head, and went out to his horse. He stood at the animal's side for a moment, gazing across at the adobe bunkhouse where the music was coming from, then he stepped across leather and went back the way he had come, bowed forward in the saddle in the teeth of the wind, eyes pinched down against stinging dust, thoughts unpleasantly grim, and the knowledge of the futility of his ride out here making him look unnaturally bitter. He reminded himself that you could lead a horse to water, but you couldn't make him drink. You could warn a man as rich and powerful as John Rockland, but you couldn't make him use good sense if he didn't want to.

The easy and logical thing would be for John

Rockland to send Dale McAfee riding. Maybe even give him a year's pay in advance and tell him to go as far as that would take him. It would save McAfee's life, and it wouldn't be any greater charity than John Rockland had done innumerable other times.

But John Rockland owned the Texas Star, the largest cow outfit in Milam County. He was rich and powerful and unafraid. No living man could tell him what he had to do.

Bannion thought of dead Alpheus King. He thought that perhaps that was just it: no living man could bring down Rockland, but a dead man might.

He went along scarcely seeing those high-overhead wind-scoured stars or the pure pewter moon. He saw little of the prairie roundabout or night's curdling shadows. He failed also to see the motionless horseman who let him pass along, then turned eastward tracing out Bannion's rearward trail until he, too, was swallowed up by the wind and dust and drenching darkness.

Bannion got back to Perdition Wells while a few lights still burned. He put up his horse, cursed the night to Sam Ryan, the night hawk, and shook grit from his clothing and spat it from his mouth. Then he strode along to the Union Eagle Saloon and pushed inside out of the wind.

Inside, he stood clear of the crowd, running his rummaging glance here and there until he found them. He noticed that instead of there being four King brothers at the bar's farthest curving, there were only three. They were turning, the three of them. Their glances came from a distance solemnly to consider Sheriff Bannion, to linger upon him.

Bannion understood at once where the fourth brother was. What he had done. Bannion wilted, and began to shoulder his way to the bar feeling weary to his spirit.

The barman showed Bannion a harassed face. "What'll it be, Sheriff?"

"Sour mash, Fred."

Bannion raised his glass when it came, emptied it in one swallow, and struck the bar with it. "Refill, Fred." He leaned there, wondering how long it would take the fourth brother to finish his trailing, assess Rockland's buildings, then return to report to the others.

The second drink came. Bannion drank this one more slowly. *Probably not long,* he thought to himself, fending off a jolly drunk who reeled against him. These were neither stupid nor procrastinating men. They did what they had to do with a minimum of wasted time. Bannion finished the drink, threw down a coin, and shook his head when Fred the barman came along and raised his eyebrows. He turned, hooked both elbows on the wood bar top, and stood there, watching the men, the girls, the poker players, and the few dancers brave enough in this shifting sharp-elbowed crowd of sweating humanity to try keeping time to the tunes of the piano player.

Then the fourth brother stepped through the yonder doors, and paused to seek his kinsmen before beginning to work his way forward. It was Al, third eldest, the one with the sheathed look of unforgiving cruelty to him. The one Bannion could not find it in his heart to condone at all.

Al sighted Bannion watching him. He pushed a blank look over to the sheriff and kept on edging through the crowd. There was no like or no dis-like in Al's gaze. There was nothing at all in the glance but recognition. Bannion might have been a once seen and now remembered horse or tree or cur dog.

Al and the others came together in that murky far corner and leaned close at the bar. Bannion knew exactly what Al was telling the others. He thought he should blame himself because Al had followed him out of town to John Rockland's Texas Star Ranch headquarters, but he did not blame himself.

This was something that Bannion was only instrumental in because his job and his badge made him so. It was not of his doing or his making. He was that chip he'd thought of earlier, being blown along against his will by a powerful circumstantial wind that he could do nothing about. He straightened up off the bar. Yes, there was one thing he could do—stay alive.

So Bannion left the Union Eagle, turned up his collar against the Santa Ana, trudged to his office, and got comfortable there. Before morning some damned fool with a soiled apron would come busting in, wringing his hands or roaring out his anger because drunk cowboys had broken some furniture or upended another cowboy in a pickle barrel of brine, or some other tomfool thing. Hell, might even report a senseless gunfight such as the one in which Dale McAfee had killed the Durham Ranch cowboy, the cause of which no one rightly knew because everyone was drunk that Saturday night, or nearly drunk.

Everyone except the old deaf swamper who had been taking away the filled spittoons and replacing them with fresh ones.

Bannion made a smoke, inhaled, and leaned far back in his chair to consider the unclean ceiling. What was it that caused the unraveling of these life patterns among men? Where was the purpose for an old derelict's killing to bring on the certain wild violence that was even now only a breath away from engulfing Perdition Wells and its countryside in a wall of devastating red flame?

The war was long over. No more than a handful of its white-thatched participants were still around. Where . . . ?

Bannion sat up with a wrench, his philosophizing ended by one fierce-stabbing thought. *How had the King brothers known their daddy was here in Perdition Wells, and who had not only known the Union Eagle's swamper as Colonel Alpheus King, but had known how to get in touch with his sons?*

Bannion's smoke went out, forgotten upon the edge of his desk. There was something here. . . . It was entirely possible some enemy of John Rockland's had done this. Rockland had his share of enemies. Maybe he even had a little of someone else's share of them—he was an arrogant man at times, a hard and forceful man of great wealth and great power.

Bannion's entire attention closed down around this one question. Who had known, and who had told?

Chapter Three

When Doyle Bannion went to the Shafter Café next morning, everything was covered over with a half inch of desert dust, but the wind had blown out and only the tan sky remained to remind him of it. He encountered Ray King and his youngest brother Austin at the counter eating breakfast hoecakes with coffee. They nodded without speaking and Bannion did the same.

He sat next to Ray King, ordered fried pork and potatoes, and said what was on the top of his mind. "You satisfied about what Al saw when he trailed me last night?"

Ray sipped coffee, then answered in his quiet voice: "We're satisfied, Mister Bannion."

"And at the saloon . . . they told you the name you wanted to know?"

"They did."

"You're satisfied there is no mistake?"

"I'm satisfied. How about you, Sheriff?"

Bannion looked over. "What do you mean?"

"I wondered why you didn't arrest this McAfee. I thought maybe it was because you weren't certain he did it." Ray King's steady, solemn eyes didn't move off Bannion. "That had to be it, Sheriff . . . you were uncertain. It couldn't have been because he's John Rockland's foreman."

Bannion let the counterman put down his plate. He eyed the food and found himself not as hungry now as he'd been earlier.

"I wasn't in the Union Eagle when that thing happened, King, but I got there about five minutes later, and I talked to just about everyone in the saloon who saw the killing of your paw. There wasn't any variation in any of those stories."

"Then you're plumb satisfied it was McAfee."

"I'm satisfied, yes. I'm also satisfied it wasn't his fault. He was defending himself at the time and your paw . . . like I told you . . . was pretty hard of hearing. Witnesses said a dozen people yelled at your paw. He evidently didn't hear . . . and that's how it happened. As for arresting Dale McAfee . . . there was no need. It's plumb legal to defend yourself in Texas, Mister King."

"No coroner's inquiry, Sheriff?"

"I'm the coroner. That's part of my job. I convened no hearing because, like I just told you, there was no need."

Austin leaned over, said something harsh to his brother, and then rose up to leave. He put his hot stare briefly, fiercely upon Bannion, then walked out of the café.

Bannion drank his cup of coffee.

"Mister King," Bannion said to Ray, "I'd like to ask you a question."

"Go right ahead, Sheriff."

"How did you know your father was here in Perdition Wells?"

"My brother Hank got a letter mailed from here."

"Did it say your father was here?"

"It did."

"Will you tell me who signed that letter?"

Ray drew his coffee cup to him and replied to this in a quiet way, saying: "No. We might need a friend here before we're finished with our business, and, as far as we know, the person who wrote that letter is the only friend we've got in Perdition Wells."

"How long had it been since you'd seen your paw?"

Ray drank some coffee, returned the cup to its saucer, before saying: "Four years."

"He didn't write?"

"No."

Bannion nodded. "He wanted to be forgotten, I'd guess. He wanted the past to die."

Ray looked at Bannion. "Did he ever tell you that?"

"No. I had no idea who he was. But I knew one thing about him. He was tired through and through. That's what I tried to tell you last night. I honestly believe, Mister King, that your father would have welcomed that bullet, if he'd had time to reflect about it. I'm absolutely convinced of it."

Ray King pushed his plate away, planted two elbows in its place on the counter, and said: "Sheriff, I figure you to be a pretty decent sort. I got that notion last night. I don't hold it against you that you went right out to warn Rockland and McAfee. But I think from today on, the less we have to say to one another the better."

Bannion called for a refill of his coffee cup. "We're not as different as you think," he told Ray King. "We believe pretty much the same about things. The only big difference is that I've lived about twenty years longer than you have. When you're my age, you'll understand what this means. Your views alter . . . you get a different insight. Right now you're thinking of only one thing . . . revenge. I'm thinking of your paw and how he would consider this thing."

"You think McAfee should get off scotfree?"

"No I don't. I don't think McAfee's conscience will let that happen as long as he lives. But I know for a fact that killing him isn't any answer."

Ray King sat on a moment, considering Bannion's face, then he arose, flung down a coin, and walked out of the café without another word.

Bannion picked at his breakfast, declared to no one—"Damn!—and also stalked out of the café without finishing the meal.

He halted upon the yonder sidewalk to look over the morning-washed roadway. There was the usual buggy and wagon traffic. Riders passed into town at both ends of it, and bonneted women with baskets on their arms were beginning the day's shopping. Across the road in front of the livery barn, next door to the Perdition Wells Stage & Freighting Company, stood the King brothers, Ray and Hank and young Austin. Al, the stone-faced brother, was not with them.

Bannion turned this over in his mind. He was beginning to understand the pattern of how these men worked. When there was some scouting to do, Al did it.

What will it be this time? Bannion considered the obvious possibilities. *Al is stalking Rockland's Texas Star . . . perhaps he's waiting for a chance to ambush Dale McAfee. No, no, that isn't it. These aren't dry-gulch killers. It's possible Al is contacting their informant, and if that is so, he is probably right here in town.*

Bannion would have traded a year off his life to know who that informant was.

He momentarily forgot about the Kings, bent to the chore of creating a cigarette, and very carefully went over in his mind everyone he could think of with whom he'd seen old Alpheus King associate.

He lit up and exhaled a big, bluish cloud. The hell of that was that Doyle Bannion, like everyone else in town, hadn't paid close attention to one old derelict. He'd seen him sitting in the sun on warm days and he'd seen him drinking an infrequent ale with some of the town's other old men, but, to his knowledge, old King had stayed pretty much to himself.

Still, there was someone hereabouts who knew what he had been. Whoever this was, he'd had to have been old King's confidant, too. Otherwise, how would he have known King had sons and where to send them a letter?

A rider swung in over at the livery barn, got down, and tossed his reins to the hostler. Then he stepped along where three other tall men sat idly looking up at him, and it was at that moment that Bannion saw that Al had returned. He watched closely, with curiosity up like a banner in his eyes, as the four King brothers sat relaxed upon that yonder bench. First they listened to Al, then quietly talked among themselves.

From that instant Bannion began to have a secret fear and a solid dislike of Al King. He smoked and looked and waited. There was nothing else he could do. He was frustrated. He couldn't arrest them because thus far they had not done anything that constituted breaking the law. Nor, in so many words, had they actually said they were going to kill Dale McAfee. He couldn't even run them out of town, and make it stick, because they hadn't disturbed the peace. In fact they hadn't even spoken to more than two or three people that Bannion knew of, and of all the people passing in and out of the stores, the saloons, the offices, not a one had any inkling that death with four different faces was sitting there relaxed in the soft sunshine of Perdition Wells' roadway.

Bannion finished his cigarette. He tossed it into the road and saw that he was under veiled scrutiny from across the way. This didn't bother him particularly. In fact, he ignored it in order to fit another piece into this puzzle. Al King had not been to see someone in town. He could have walked anywhere within pistol shot easier than he could have ridden, and therefore he hadn't been in town, he'd been out on the range somewhere. Bannion thought that "somewhere" was the Texas Star.

He was still thinking this when seven horsemen, riding in a bunch, came swinging in from the east. They slowed with range dust settling behind them where they struck the main roadway, and came along at a deliberate walk.

Bannion recognized John Rockland, and turned cold in the guts. He had his answer about Al now. He'd been out scouting, had seen these Texas Star men, and had come back at once to report to the others.

Rockland was astride a fine, blood bay horse with a wavy black mane. He looked good on a horse any time, but, sitting his carved saddle now, a foot or two ahead of his range crew, John Rockland appeared as something special.

Bannion shot his onward glance to Rockland's

men. Normally when the entire crew came to town, there were eight of them, including Rockland. The missing man, Bannion saw at once and with great relief, was Dale McAfee.

Across the way the four tall King men were sitting easy, with legs pushed far out, hats tilted forward to shield faces from warming sunlight, watching Rockland's Texas Star advance steadily southward without speaking or moving their eyes or gun hands.

Bannion could feel a curdling of the atmosphere. Others, the length of the roadway, also saw those riding men and began to look, to wonder, to speak back and forth about this, perhaps also feeling something indefinable but jarring in the air.

Rockland saw Bannion and reined over. Behind him sat his riders, their attention holding to the sheriff, too, their backs squarely to the Kings.

Rockland nodded. He was distant this morning, distant and impersonally unapproachable. His nod meant nothing and he wasted no time with amenities. He said: "Did you take care of that matter we discussed last night, Bannion?"

Bannion, sensing John Rockland's coldness, tried to keep hostility from his answer, but made no effort to keep out the irony. "No I didn't, Mister Rockland, and, as a matter of fact, you just put your back to the four of them."

Rockland didn't move for what seemed a long

while. He regarded Bannion from eyes that grew misty with antagonism, then he gently raised his rein hand and turned his horse. He pushed past those crowding riders, and halted where he had a good view of the four men watching him impassively from the battered bench between the livery barn and the stage office. He nodded. None of the Kings nodded back or moved a muscle.

"I'm John Rockland," he said, and let it lie there for a second before continuing. "I think you must be the King brothers." None of the big men acted as though they had heard. Rockland's pause this time was longer. Bannion could see the big vein in the side of his neck swelling.

"Well, are you the King brothers or aren't you?"

Hank answered, saying simply: "You're the one who's got something to say, Rockland. Get on with it."

Bannion saw the back of John Rockland's neck turn dark red. He could not see Rockland's face but he could plainly hear his voice, and that was just as good, for the words fell like steel balls striking glass now.

"I've heard why you're here," Rockland said. "That killing was a very unfortunate thing, but it was purest accident. Everyone is sorry about it. That's going to be the end of it. Your father is dead and buried. He can't be brought back and the wisest thing for you to do is saddle up and ride back where you came from."

A man came up beside Doyle Bannion, reached out to catch his attention, and said in a whisper: "What's going on?"

Bannion said fiercely: "Shut up!" It wasn't until then was he conscious that people were standing like statues on both sides of the roadway, watching as this drama unfolded. The bystanders were captivated, gripped by the stillness, the mortal hush that filled in after Rockland stopped speaking, waiting and scarcely breathing, for an answer from those four big men.

It was Al who spoke. With something very close to scorn in his voice, he said: "Why didn't you bring McAfee with you? But you should know that talking won't change anything. Just send McAfee into town. Or maybe the lot of you'd like to come in with him. That's all we want . . . so go on away, Rockland, unless you're buying into this, too, because we're not a damn' bit interested in you . . . or your riders." Al paused, then concluded with: "Make it easy or make it hard . . . it's up to you. Send McAfee in and he can take his pick which of us he wants to meet. That way only one or two men'll die. That'll be the easy way." Al paused briefly before continuing. "You buy in, Rockland, and pay your riders a bonus so they'll also buy in, and things won't be so simple for any of us. That way, we figure, maybe a half dozen or even a dozen men'll die. It's up to you."

John Rockland sat there with his distant, withdrawn look, regarding the four Kings from a face iron-like and unafraid. "Maybe Bannion didn't tell you," he said, "but I protect my own. That goes for McAfee, too."

Ray King spoke for the first time. "I'm not surprised about that. I got the impression the way you rode into town you'd be the kind who'd protect a murderer, Rockland. I've seen a dozen just like you across Texas. Big men, powerful men, above the law and beyond it. All right. You called the tune, we didn't. You want to dance, so I reckon you'll just have to pay the musicians."

Ray stood up. He walked fifty feet to the south. Hank got up, also. He passed fifty feet to John Rockland's right. Young Austin, the fiery, proud, and fearless one, walked dead ahead and halted three feet in front of John Rockland's handsome blood bay gelding. His pale eyes were fully settled upon the owner of Texas Star.

Al, the one Bannion watched next, went along to the livery barn door and faded from sight around it.

Something like a sigh passed up and down the roadway. Men turned, took the women with them, and passed without delay into whatever store was nearest. In a twinkling the main roadway of Perdition Wells was empty except for Doyle Bannion, the thoroughly exposed Texas Star men on their unmoving horses, and those three visible and one invisible big man from west Texas.

It was very clear to Doyle Bannion that John Rockland had not expected it to come to this so quickly. In fact, Bannion began to feel that Rockland probably had thought, up until Hank King had spoken, that his name, his known wealth and power, would do the whole thing for him.

Now that it hadn't, Bannion wished he dared move, dared go down into the roadway and walk along until he could turn and see up into John Rockland's face. To his knowledge this was the first time he'd ever heard of Rockland being called in his own town, with his crew around him, and with a gun on his hip.

"We're waiting," Ray King called softly, and said no more.

A cowboy near Bannion said into the ensuing silence: "Hold it, fellers. Hold it just a minute. I'm paid to work cattle, not fight no wars. I'm goin' to turn south and ride off down that damned road and I'll have both hands plumb in plain sight."

Bannion looked at the cowhand who made the announcement. He was a raffish-looking rider who hadn't been working for Texas Star very long, and he now did exactly as he'd said. He worked his horse out of the crowd around him, reined southward, and walked along with both elbows held out wide and both gloved hands up in plain sight.

"Me, too," said another man. This one rode southward, too.

Bannion could not place this man. He had to be a new rider, but Bannion could, and did, step forward now, since that hush and stillness was broken. He walked along until he was able to turn and see Rockland's face as well as the faces of his remaining riders, and halt there. He was a little distance to one side of Austin King.

Bannion knew what he was going to say. He knew, too, that Rockland was going to obey him because no man set to fight ever waited this long to do it. The longer Rockland sat there trying to make his decision, the less was the likelihood of there being a shoot-out.

"Mister Rockland," Bannion declared. "Lead out with your men and head for home. At any rate get out of Perdition Wells."

Rockland shifted his attention. His eyes had no expression, only a peculiar shininess. He considered Doyle Bannion for a moment, then, without speaking or looking back, he reined his horse northward and started along.

Four Texas Star riders went slowly out of town behind their employer. Two of these men were old Texas Star hands. They twisted to glare backward because this town had been theirs a hundred times. They had treed its citizens and shot out its lights; they had brawled in its saloons and run the riders of other cow outfits out of it in a shower of lead. This exodus now was the bitterest humiliation either of them had ever experienced. It was like poison in their minds and acid in their bellies.

Bannion watched these two men in particular. It would only take one wrong move to start gunfire even yet. He remained in the roadway's center until those two bleak-eyed men were shut off by a building, then he turned, saw that the four King brothers were back by their bench, standing solemnly, watching him, saying nothing, and seemingly unaffected by the near thing they had just passed through.

Bannion went up to them. He stopped and looked into each of the four faces.

The Kings returned this prolonged regard. They showed no fear, no paleness at all.

"You think that ended it?" Bannion asked.

Ray King shook his head; the others said nothing. Al sat down on the bench and began examining his fingernails. Austin went over to stand behind him, ignoring the sheriff to glance along the roadway where people were standing in little clutches heatedly talking and looking occasionally up where Bannion stood facing those four big men.

"That only started it, and the advice Rockland gave you was plenty sound," the sheriff added.

"It probably was," Ray responded in his soft way of speaking. "Only we're not here for advice, Sheriff."

"Some big man," muttered young Austin, contempt dripping from these words, and grunted his disdain to Bannion. "What's everyone hereabouts think so highly of him for, I'd like to know."

Bannion continued to regard Ray. "You're not so young," he said.

Ray nodded, saying quietly: "I'm not underestimating him, Sheriff. Not at all. But nothing's changed. I'm only sorry McAfee wasn't with him, otherwise the whole thing would be over with now."

"Yeah," Bannion said fiercely, "and maybe the lot of you wouldn't be riding home, either."

Al looked up. "Sheriff, you worry too much. Now I got a feeling Mister Rockland's going to get rid of McAfee like he was a jinx, and you won't have to worry about any of this any more."

Bannion regarded Al for a long time, then he walked away without another word to any of them.

He was almost to his office when he was stopped by a heavy-set older man with a cowman's ruddy complexion and perpetually narrowed eyes.

"What's going on?" the man asked. "I just rode in. The damned town acts like someone just run up and down the road dragging a bag full of skunks behind his horse."

Bannion said tartly: "John, that rider of yours

41

who shot it out with Dale McAfee did more harm by dying . . . accidentally . . . then he'd have done if he'd killed Rockland's foreman." Bannion started past.

The rough-looking old cowman hooked his arm, bringing his around. "Doyle, who are those four big fellers up there?"

"Those are the King brothers. They just backed John Rockland down and his whole Texas Star crew."

The cowman's grip tightened on Bannion's arm. He began to smile flintily. "Tell me about it, Doyle."

"Come in the office."

Chapter Four

Rugged Clell Durham was a free-graze cowman; that is, he owned no land in the county. He bought big steers in early spring and grazed them over unclaimed range until their weight gain was sufficient to make him a good profit, then he trailed them to rail's end and shipped them to whatever beef market was paying well. His breed of Texas cowman was fast becoming extinct because fences were coming and also because big ranchers such as John Rockland were building empires of deeded land.

That had been the actual reason for the shoot-out between Durham's Box D cowboy and Rockland's ranch foreman at the Union Eagle. Antagonism existed between free-graze men and established land-owning cattlemen.

Durham, holding the killing of his rider against Rockland even more than against McAfee, the actual killer, heard all that Doyle Bannion had to tell him, and was pleased about it. He left Bannion's office with a springy step, went up where the King brothers were sitting silently in the sun, and introduced himself. He then explained about his dead rider, and launched into a good offer of employment. He was certain, because Rockland's power was great, that these four big men would join forces with him and be delighted for the opportunity. He could see that these were not ordinary men. They would be smart enough to know that four men by themselves could not hope to stand against Rockland's Texas Star.

But grizzled old Durham got a surprise. Ray King told him he didn't believe he and his brothers wanted jobs right now. Maybe later, after they'd taken care of some personal business.

Durham's anticipation wilted. "Listen, boys, Doyle Bannion just told me your story and how you run Rockland out of his town. Take my advice and make some friends, fast."

"You got an axe to grind?" asked Al King. "We're obliged for your offer, mister, but we fight our own battles and I guess you'll have to fight yours."

Durham said a sharp word. "Two of Rockland's men quit him. He'll replace 'em with gunmen, now he knows he's got a battle on his hands."

"Mister Durham," Ray said in his deceptively mild way, "you want guns for a range war with Texas Star. Go somewhere else to get them. We don't want to start any range war. We just want one man . . . and we'll get him."

Durham snorted. "Like hell you will. From this morning on Dale McAfee won't be alone, even when he beds down."

"We know about that," Austin King said, showing his short temper to Durham. "We'll mind our business and you mind yours, Mister Durham. You got your war bonnet set for Rockland . . . do what you got to do. Just keep your nose out of our affairs."

Durham teetered there, looking at those four men. He twisted a little at the sound of approaching footsteps, saw Sheriff Bannion coming up, and said in parting: "All right, fellers, but when the smoke clears away, those of you who survive come see me." Then Durham hastened away.

Bannion watched the free-graze cowman turn in at the saddle shop nearby. His gaze was ironic. Without looking down, he said to the Kings: "He try to hire you boys?"

Hank King nodded. The others paid no attention to Bannion.

"It makes me think more of you that none of you took him up on it."

"We're not here to get involved in a range war," said Ray. "He's got his problem and we got ours. What he does about his is none of our affair . . . and we don't need him to take care of our problem."

Bannion shot a sidelong glance at the sun. It was nearing high noon. "You're going to get a big dose of Rockland medicine, I think, unless you get some common sense about that problem of yours, though," Bannion said. "You should know that

Rockland told me to run you fellers out of town."

Hank, who was trimming fingernails with a sharp Barlow knife, snapped the thing closed and pocketed it. "That wouldn't change anything," he told Bannion. "This way, at least we're where you can see us. The other way, we'd camp up some arroyo somewhere, you wouldn't know where we were . . . and we'd still get McAfee."

Ray stood up suddenly. He was tired of this conversation. It showed in the way he looked beyond Bannion at store fronts, at roadway traffic, and strolling pedestrians.

Finally he said: "If I'd been Rockland, Sheriff, I'd never have done what he did this morning, because now we know every man who works for him by sight. A man can't surprise his enemies by revealing who his hired hands are."

"Not all of them," retorted Bannion. "He's got a crippled-up old range rider who is the ranch cook."

Ray looked at Bannion, then he said—"Come on."—to his brothers and the four of them hiked out into the roadway bound for the Union Eagle.

Bannion watched them go. He watched them halt outside the saloon doors, speak briefly together, then only three of them pushed on inside.

Al King stepped back to the plank walk's edge, leaned there against an upright with his thumbs hooked into his shell belt, and kept a solemn watch as Bannion turned to saunter into the stage office. When Bannion was out of sight, Al stepped back down into the roadway, trudged to the livery barn, and five minutes later rode out the back way, heading north.

Bannion left the stage office, hurried out the back way, and passed along northward to the stable, also. There, he rigged out his saddle animal, sprang astride, and rode out into the rear alleyway, heading north.

A man, once understanding the stratagems of other men, is a fool only if he doesn't profit by what he's observed. Doyle Bannion was far from a fool. A philosophical man he was and a tolerant man he might be, but a fool he was not, regardless of what Al King and perhaps Austin King thought of him.

In broad daylight upon the Texas plains it required a seasoned and wily tracker to trail another man without being seen. Because there were no trees worth the name, no hills or land swells or ridges in the correct direction or in any sufficient profusion, an experienced desert horseman borrowed a leaf from the book of the prairie Indians. He made his careful way through the thorn-pin brush, the chaparral, sage, bitter brush, and also through places where deep shadows lay. He moved steadily only when it was completely safe to do so, and he sometimes sat without moving a muscle for as long as ten minutes before crossing an area where unavoidable sun smash glittered, waiting to reveal his movement forward.

Bannion knew these tricks and a bagful of other ones just as useful. And today he used most of them in order to keep Al King in sight. He also had another useful advantage. After a mile of trailing, he knew from the direction in which King was riding that he was making for one of the holding grounds where Texas Star cattle were worked this time of year.

It was not difficult from this to surmise King's purpose, either. He knew enough about the four west Texas brothers to attribute motive to Al's steady onward riding.

Another mile forward, then a third one, and Al drew into the north-south run of a cutbank arroyo. Here, he disappeared entirely and because Al could not see out any more than Bannion could see in, the sheriff was able to lope ahead into a bois d'arc thicket and take his position there in perfect safety.

Al rode up out of that arroyo at its northernmost end. He was on the lee side of a little hill where some red bark grew. Bannion saw him get down, tie his horse, and ascend the little hill, get down on his belly up there and lie perfectly motionless for a long time, gazing ahead at that holding ground.

Bannion had his answer, but he lingered until long after King had gone back to his horse, got astride, and turned to go back toward Perdition

Wells. Then Bannion also climbed that hill and lay down.

Ahead a long quarter mile was a Texas Star ranch wagon, a little ragged smoke from a fresh-laid cooking fire, and the strewn bedrolls and camp gear of several riders. There were six men gathered there, evidently newly arrived at this place because they had not yet off-saddled. They were hunkering near the wagon, smoking and conversing. Behind them, at the wagon's tailgate, was Texas Star's ranch cook, a soiled flour sack lashed about his middle, working over a big pan.

One of those men in the wagon shade caught and held Bannion's attention. He knew this rider by his wide hat and his ivory-butted six-gun. He also knew that Al King had identified this man by the simple process of elimination. As Ray had said, the Kings now knew Rockland's riders by sight. It had been no great thing for Al, lying there ticking off the men he recognized as men he'd seen with John Rockland in town, to ascertain that the one man he did not recognize was Dale McAfee.

Bannion got up and started back for his horse.

The hell of it was—Al King was perfectly correct. That man with the ivory-butted gun and wide-brimmed black hat *was* Dale McAfee.

Bannion worked clear of the bois d'arc thicket and saw Al King off in the hazy distance. Slowly he eased out in the identical direction, not really

49

caring now whether he was seen or not. He did not ride fast.

He arrived back at Perdition Wells with the dying day's sun turning its increasing red light over the town near to suppertime, giving those bleached and warped buildings a benign and hospitable appearance that they did not really possess at all.

He put up his animal and crossed to the Shafter Café for supper—in the cow country supper was the last meal of the day while dinner was the noon meal. Being a bachelor, Doyle Bannion was a steady customer at this café—the cleanest in town, which actually wasn't saying a whole lot—but also like a bachelor, he ate to keep body and soul united. There was no other reason to eat. Restaurant food being palatable to the starving, the needy, and the unattached, it was never more than an expedient to the discerning. Bannion, the single man, could lay no claim to discernment in this matter, nor did he.

He walked inside, nodded to several men at a table on his left, went to the counter, and sat down, at the same time pushing back his hat and looking around. His gaze crossed the steady regard of the King brothers at a table. He nodded, they nodded, and Bannion settled around calling for fried steak, a side order of Sonora onions, black coffee, and apple pie. He did not feel particularly elated, but he did feel that he was beginning to get his teeth into the dilemma of Colonel King's sons, and John Rockland's Texas Star outfit. Of one thing he was now certain. Al King had been sent to locate Dale McAfee for simply one reason. He had located him and now the four men from west Texas would saddle up and ride out to do what they felt they had to do.

Bannion had observed how those four men operated and he also understood their complete fearlessness. Finally, he knew they wasted no time, were minimal and sparing in movement and speech. These were the facets that enabled him now to enjoy the first meal he'd sat down to since they'd ridden into Perdition Wells the night before, because he could assess the actions and reactions of these big men, and he could accordingly plan his own actions.

Both in the café and later, out upon the walkways when he was making his routine rounds, it was clear to Bannion that the townspeople of Perdition Wells had viewed the rebuff of John Rockland as some kind of a crisis, some kind of a challenge to the established order of existence. While he knew perfectly well that Rockland had many enemies in town because of his personal aloofness and the swaggering boldness of the Texas Star men, they still preferred these known things to the unknown things represented by the four King brothers.

Bannion was accosted for his views, for his

reasons for not running the Kings out of Perdition Wells, and, by those who secretly hoped Rockland's fall was imminent, for his proposed course of action in the face of this fresh support for Rockland's enemies.

Bannion's answers were usually the same. He could not, according to law, do anything until an infraction of the law had actually been committed, but he did not mean to stand by and see a war start here, either. About how he thought he might prevent this, Bannion said nothing because he did not know himself how he could prevent it. All he knew—and he kept this strictly to himself—was that he knew John Rockland, and he was beginning to know the King brothers. These things were in his favor if nothing else seemed to be. But Doyle Bannion was no coward. He would move and move hard, when he thought it was time to do so.

Chapter Five

Only fools duplicate their mistakes. Bannion loafed in town until sunset came and went. He visited the Union Eagle, saw the King brothers there having a casual drink, and went at once to the livery barn, saddled up, and rode out of town through back alleyways. A mile on, Bannion dismounted, pressed his ear to the ground—to make certain he was not being followed—and rode the balance of the way to John Rockland's house in a loose lope.

Across from Rockland's handsome wood house, faint orange light showed at the Texas Star bunkhouse. Bannion saw a shadow pass behind a window there and was turning to tie his mount at the stud post, when out of the porch shadows a white blur of movement came toward him. Bannion drew upright, wondering whether this was Rockland's wife or daughter. He knew them both. They were very handsome women of the long-legged, high-breasted Southern breed.

It was Judith, the daughter. She stopped near Bannion with star shine lying like dull gold upon her blonde hair, with her gun-metal gray eyes steady, and her beautiful face very solemn.

"Good evening, Sheriff," she said. "My father

hasn't returned from the range yet. He rode out to the holding ground this afternoon. There's going to be a drive soon, to rail's end."

"Hello, Miss Judy," Bannion responded, and smiled, gaining a little time to adjust his thoughts to what suddenly had become a crisis. He had come here to induce Rockland to bring McAfee in from the holding grounds and keep him at the ranch for a couple of days.

"Sorry your paw isn't here. I wanted to talk to him."

"Talk to me, Sheriff," said the lovely girl, keeping that disconcertingly level gaze upon Bannion. "I heard what happened in town this morning. Old Rufus got it from the men and told me."

"Rufus," Bannion said, still half smiling, "is an inveterate old gossip."

"But an accurate one, Sheriff."

Rufus Paige was Texas Star's ranch cook. He'd broken both legs under a falling horse years before, and with the advent of age the stiffness resulting from this injury had reduced him from a range rider to chore man, and finally to ranch cook. Rufus had one periodic weakness—twice-annual drunks of prodigious proportions—and he was, at times, a garrulous gossip. Generally, though, he was well liked. John Rockland kept Rufus on a kind of pension. He had to work only when he wished to, and his aberrations were religiously overlooked. Rufus had been almost a father to Judith Rockland during her early years when John Rockland was away with cattle drives laying the foundation of his fortune. Bannion, as well as almost everyone else, knew how close the old man and this beautiful girl were.

Bannion said now: "Miss Judy, if old Rufus told you about what happened in town, he probably also heard why it happened and told you that, too."

"Yes, he did." Judy put her head a little to one side. "That's why you're out here tonight, isn't it?"

"Yes."

"Will you tell me, Sheriff?"

"If you'll promise me two things, Miss Judy. One, that you won't tell Rufus, because, if you do, he'll tell your paw's riders and that would upset everything. And two, that you'll send someone to fetch your paw home so I can talk to him."

Judith nodded. "I won't tell Rufus. But I have a better idea about the other thing. I'll take your message to my father. That way you won't have to wait around here until he gets back."

Bannion considered this, found it acceptable, and said: "I want him to bring Dale McAfee back from the holding ground and keep him here at the ranch for a few days."

"Yes, I see," John Rockland's beautiful daughter responded in a speculative tone. "You think those men in town will find McAfee at the camp and kill him there."

"I don't think that, Miss Judy . . . I know it. One of them slipped out there today and located McAfee. Then he rode back and told the others."

"Are you sure, Sheriff?"

"I'm sure, Miss Judy. I trailed him there and back."

"Sheriff, what kind of men are these King brothers?"

Bannion lifted his shoulders and let them fall. "Men," he said succinctly. "Just men."

"Gunmen?"

Bannion pursed his lips over this. He scowled faintly. "Well, no, Miss Judy. Clell Durham tried to hire them to fight your paw today and they wouldn't do it. No, I wouldn't call them gunfighters exactly, but I wouldn't call 'em just plain cowboys, either. They look plenty capable . . . plenty able to hold their own in any kind of company. I'd say they're determined men." Bannion's face brightened. "You heard why they're here? Who their paw was?"

"Yes."

"Well, I'd say they're fit sons for Colonel King of King's Confederate Raiders. There's no fear in 'em anywhere, Miss Judy, and they're men who don't talk a lot. They keep to themselves."

"Can't you arrest them?"

Bannion removed his hat and minutely examined

it before he answered this. "They haven't done anything."

"They called my father this morning, didn't they?"

"Well, not exactly. He called them, Miss Judy. He rode up and told them it'd be best if they got out of town."

Rockland's daughter looked away, ran her gaze out over the yard toward the gloomy west. Her delicate dark brows curved inward and downward. She said: "Sheriff . . ."

"Yes, Miss Judy?"

"Could I talk to them . . . reason with them?"

Bannion looked surprised. He gently shook his head. "What could you say? I've reasoned with them. Your paw made it plenty plain what would happen if they didn't give it up. They're doing what they believe is right. A bullet might stop them . . . but words won't." Bannion shifted his weight; he felt an urge to say something gallant. He saw her beauty and her ripeness there in that soft-lighted night, and Bannion was still young enough to admire both deeply. He said: "There's not a living man who wouldn't listen to you . . . not if he had two good eyes and red blood in his veins. But I'm afraid beauty isn't enough this time."

Judy turned her gaze back to Bannion. She sent him a little twinkling smile, but there was an iron-like hardness in the depths of that look.

"The worst that could happen is that I'll fail," she said, "and, if that's the case, nothing will be changed anyway, will it?"

"No, Miss Judy, I reckon not."

Bannion's attention was diverted by the sound of a horse slowly pacing its way southward from Texas Star's immense log barn. He listened, thinking this might be John Rockland returning, then it dawned on him that whoever this horseman was, he was traveling away from the ranch, not toward it. He recalled seeing a shadow of a man pass behind the bunkhouse window and figured the rider must be this cowboy. Then he saw the flare of a match upon the bunkhouse porch, the afterward glow of a cigarette tip, and what seemed initially to be an insignificant thing came to be a little mystery to him. The rider on the porch, the beautiful girl in front of him, seemed to be the only people at Texas Star this night. Who, then, was the night rider?

With her eyes watching Bannion's face, Judy said: "It's probably Rufus. Don't look so suspicious, Sheriff." She made a low little chuckle. "Does law work make men so quick to notice things?"

Bannion looked down. He was thinking of the many times he'd hauled Rufus Paige off to jail to sober up, and of how Rufus had violently protested being sent back to Texas Star on horseback, because he said riding pained him.

He brought up a smile to match Judith's smile. "That's something law work sure enough does," he murmured, and turned to untie his horse. "Will you ride out and tell your paw what I said?"

"Right away, Sheriff. It's such a beautiful night I was thinking of going out to meet him, anyway."

Bannion stepped up, put his hat back on, and flashed the girl one last wide smile. "Perdition Wells isn't a wild place, but all the same I'd better get back."

Bannion left the Texas Star riding slowly. He did not ride southeasterly as was customary, to strike the stage road and plod along it into town. Instead, he angled around until he was heading due south in the wake of that Texas Star horseman, and as he'd done once before this day, he kept his goodly distance to avoid detection, and from time to time he dismounted to hug the earth listening for, and hearing, the steady, slow, and onward pace of that other man in the night.

Bannion was piqued. If this was indeed old Rufus, it would certainly have to be something quite vital to make him ride as he was now riding, but if it wasn't Rufus—who was it? John Rockland and his working crew were at the holding ground. Judith and that solitary rider were back at the ranch. The only person unaccounted for was Judith's mother. Bannion put that thought out of his mind at once.

It had to be Rufus.

Bannion saw, faint and hull-down upon the black horizon, Perdition Wells' lights. He was perplexed and almighty curious. He dismounted and walked with his saddle animal, stopping more frequently now to listen for that onward horse-man. Old Rufus was curving a little westerly now, but he was not heading for the heart of town, at all.

Bannion was a half mile closer to town when it began to occur to him that Rufus was not making for Perdition Wells at all. He was heading for a small hill east of town a mile or so. This made no sense at all. From that little hill a person got a good sighting of the village, but other than that . . .

The graveyard!

Atop that hill, enclosed within a wrought-iron fence, was the cemetery of Perdition Wells. Bannion stopped cold. He stood like stone for a full minute, then got down flat, and lay there a long time, listening to those diminishing onward reverberations. He eventually stood up solemnly to brush himself off, his expression blank and instinctively knowing.

He went on as far as a chaparral stand, tied his animal there, and then went the balance of that little distance on foot. Near the rise of cemetery hill Bannion got down upon his knees, cocked his head, and watched that horseman breast the skyline, his shape darker than the roundabout night. He watched the man dismount with recognizable ungainliness, stand a moment flexing his legs, then tie the horse to the iron fence and hobble along to the graveyard's gate and pass inside.

It was without any doubt, Rufus Paige.

Bannion started uphill with extreme care, feeling his way so as not to make a sound. He was near enough to Rufus's tied horse to reach forth and touch the animal, when he heard a shod hoof somewhere on the little hill's southerly slope strike stone. Bannion dropped flat, waiting to skyline this second horseman. He saw the dark-cut head and shoulders first, then the man's broad chest and narrow waist. Then both horse and rider were upon the top out, halted. Bannion let his breath out in a silent, long sigh. He let that second man also dismount and secure his animal before dropping back downhill a ways and gliding forward toward the gate. He was belly down and blending into the night no more than fifty feet away when that second man passed into the cemetery with a long stride and identifiable grace that almost at once faded out in the darkness.

Bannion darted to the gate, passed through, and made for a large, ornate, and very old monument. He got behind this, scarcely breathing. Somewhere on eastward, came the murmur of men's lowered tones.

Bannion knew this graveyard well. He moved

carefully from headstone to headstone, passing always closer to where those voices emanated. He stopped and doubled far over, when those voices abruptly ceased. He waited, pain beginning to grow in his back, unmindful of this, until the voices began again. Then Bannion got behind another of the man-high stones, and straightened up. A hundred feet ahead were the two men. One was recognizable by his height, his easy posture, and his way of thoughtfully standing with his head lowered. The second silhouette was supporting himself with an outflung arm, his hips against the iron fence, and his head tilted up now with faint night light touching it. The man was easily identifiable at once as Rufus Paige.

Bannion strained to hear. Now, though, the men were only sporadically speaking, their voices turned low, turned solemn and muted. Bannion could not distinguish what was being said.

He tried for a time to catch some inkling of this dwindling conversation, then, resigned to failure at this, he sat down upon the ground and undertook to organize his own thoughts. He was deterred here, though, when the two conspirators suddenly left their position near the easterly iron fence and began to pace along, side-by-side, back toward the gate.

Bannion considered rising up to confront them. In the end he did not do this, but he did get up to his feet after they had faded out westward.

He cut across the ground to the northward fence where Rufus had left his horse, climbed over it, and dropped back down again to wait.

It was a long wait. Rufus did not appear for a full fifteen minutes. Bannion watched his approach, noted how the crippled man seemed to make slow and painful progress, then he rose up on the near side of the horse and stood there with pale moonlight showing his expression of hard suspicion, waiting for the ranch cook to see him.

Rufus bent to untie his horse. He turned, flung up one of his split reins, minced along the animal's left side with his head down, reached for the stirrup, and brought his head up. He was staring straight into Doyle Bannion's eyes.

For the space of a long withheld breath neither man moved nor blinked. Then Sheriff Bannion hooked his thumbs into his shell belt and nodded.

"Hello, Rufus. You're quite a piece from home, aren't you?"

The older man let go his stirrup. He rocked back a little with purest astonishment upon his face. He opened his lips and closed them.

"That grave you were standing by . . . over there along the east fence . . . belongs to an old feller about your age named King. I didn't know you knew Alpheus King, Rufus."

John Rockland's cook stood like stone. He was holding that one split rein and staring. It took a full minute for his surprise to pass, then his shoulders

63

settled lower and his eyes lost their wideness.

"You got a lot o' nerve," he said, his tone breathless and unsteady, "spyin' on folks in the night, Doyle Bannion."

Bannion let this pass. "Why did you do it, Rufus? Why did you write those boys about their paw's killing?"

"Who says I did?"

"I do. Dog-gone you, Rufus, don't you lie to me. Why didn't you let the thing end here?"

"Because Dale McAfee ain't fit to have Colonel King wipe his feet on him, that's why."

Bannion nodded. He had this much of the mystery worked out already. He also thought he had more of it worked out, too. Seeking support for this other idea, he said: "You served under him, didn't you?"

"Yes. And, by God, I'm proud of it, too. I was his forage master. I was a captain in King's Confederate Raiders. Now you go ahead an' make something out o' that, Doyle Bannion!"

"No," the sheriff replied quietly, "I won't make anything out of it, Rufus. I'm just old enough to remember how it was after the war."

"You think you know," Rufus said with bitterness. "You think you know, Doyle, but you don't. Hunted like animals, prices on our heads, scairt to lie down at night without a brace o' cocked pistols to hand. Running night an' day. You think you know. . . ."

Bannion went over to the iron fence. He leaned against it. "You shouldn't have done it though, Rufus."

"Give me one good reason why I shouldn't have. Just one!"

"Because the colonel wouldn't have wanted it to end like this. That's one reason. Another one is because, by bringing his sons here, you've resurrected a lot of the old bitterness . . . you've made it just about certain that some men are going to die."

"Dale McAfee's going to die, you mean. He deserves to an' you damn' well know it, Sheriff. He didn't have to kill the colonel. He didn't have to shoot at all, only he's mean an' lowdown like a sidewinder, drunk or sober. He saw the colonel behind that Box D cowboy. He just didn't give a damn, so he fired."

Bannion turned and looked steadily into Rufus Paige's muddy old eyes, saw the ferocity there and said no more. These old men from another time were a different breed. What they held to be right, they willingly died to preserve. No one ever talked them out of a principle. Bannion knew he could not talk this old man out of his convictions. He pushed off the fence.

"Go home, Rufus. This has been a long ride for you. Good night."

Bannion started down off cemetery hill toward his horse.

Chapter Six

Doyle Bannion made a bad mistake, but he knew nothing of it until the following morning. It was a common mistake. An error of underestimation. He had not thought, when he'd ridden out of Perdition Wells to induce John Rockland to keep Dale McAfee at the headquarters ranch, that the King brothers were set to strike. Perhaps he should have known that. In the after years he thought often that he certainly should have. But a man's conscience is more nagging than a wife and usually it is about as lacking in understanding as well.

Bannion hadn't been gone from Perdition Wells twenty minutes when all four of the King brothers walked out of the Union Eagle, got their saddled horses from the livery barn, and struck out northward in a tight group.

Around them lay the prairie, the silence of this night, and the softly lighted silvery gloom. The moon was a quarter full and tipped. There was a blue-white blaze of stars and an arched vault of soft, deep purple stretching from earth's unseen curving in all directions to the greatest height of infinity.

They traveled in full silence, having no need

for talk, with cold, impersonal Al King leading the way upon his big Roman-nosed buckskin horse, pacing off the open miles and thinking ahead to what must be done.

All the decisions had been made, and Austin, the youngest, rode now with destiny beside him and his seasoned gun hand lying easy upon a saddle swell. Unless McAfee said differently, it would be young Austin King, fiercest of the lot, who McAfee would face this night.

They by-passed the north-south arroyo Al had earlier ridden into and up out of. They got to the bois d'arc thicket where Sheriff Bannion had tied his horse. They sat a moment, gauging the night for sounds, heard only the bawl of a cow somewhere distant and the shrill answer from her calf, and they dismounted, tied their beasts, and went as far as the pale plain. There they halted again to let Al take the lead up that little onward ridge.

From their achieved eminence the four west Texans looked down where a little fire burned, saw those ringed-around faces at that fire, and paused just long enough to exchange a silent look among themselves, then they split up, going forward and downward in four different directions.

At John Rockland's holding grounds seven men sat relaxed with firelight shadowing their countenances with its constant writhing. Some of them smoked. Some sat with drooping eyes. All of them were lounging in that good comfort that range men seek with day's ending, their cares for this little time forgotten, their muscles all loose and soft, their bellies pleasantly glowing from sourdough bread, beans, and black coffee.

"They'll be west toward the old Comanche burial ground," said a sprawled rider, speaking of the cattle they would begin to round up when dawn came again. "I seen a lot of 'em over there last month when I was . . ."

"Naw," interrupted a narrow-faced, cold-eyed man with a black hat pushed back and an ivory-butted gun lashed to his leg. "Hell, Ira, last month might as well have been last summer. They're over by the hot springs, east of here."

"You know that for a fact?" Ira said, lifting his eyes and sounding nettled.

Dale McAfee shrugged, contemptuous of the cowboy's irritation. He was a good man with a gun and they all knew it. Also, he was John Rockland's range boss. Ira's anger would subside from the weight of these two considerations.

"I don't know it, but I'll lay you a little bet."

Ira hung fire over his reply to this as another man spoke up: "Rider coming."

John Rockland, who was squatting next to his foreman, jerked his head up and around, showing that something other than this idle campfire talk was in his mind. He got up and stood looking, his square jaw and high-bridged nose hawk-like in that reddish glow.

Several of the others also rose up. Among them was Dale McAfee. That earlier quietude vanished in an instant. Every man among them was suddenly alert and wary, in each of their minds the same bleak thoughts.

A man farther back than the others blew out his breath. "It's Miss Judy," he said, sounding relieved.

Rockland went past to meet the rider, his face turning a little unpleasant because he was running two thoughts together and totaling them unpleasantly.

"What are you doing out here?" he said at once, when Judith reined down. "It's not a good idea for you to be riding around alone in the night, Judy."

She sat for a moment, looking at her father. Then she swung down without speaking and gazed at the other faces. Some of that earlier tenseness lingered in the eyes of the men and around their flattened lips. She saw this, understood the reason for it, and even felt a little of that apprehension herself.

"I came out to ride back with you," she finally said to her father.

One of the men, an old Texas Star hand, stooped, caught up a metal pot, and filled a tin cup with black coffee. He smiled at Judy and held the cup out to her.

She took it, saying: "Jack, you're a gentleman."

The old rider's rough, weathered face creased into a hundred deep wrinkles and his square white teeth flashed.

"Are you ready to go back now?" she asked her father over the cup's rim, watching him closely. "I want to talk to you."

John Rockland looked around, shrugged, and said: "I suppose so, honey. Ira, fetch my horse, will you?" He stood looking at his men.

They returned his look. Something passed back and forth, something masculine and solid. Then Ira came on with Rockland's animal, and the owner of Texas Star stepped up. Judy handed back her coffee cup and mounted, also. The men watched how she did this with strong approval. Judith Rockland was a fit daughter for her father. Along with his gun-metal eyes, she had his poise and his strength. They waved when Judith waved and stood on, watching those two people jog southward down a black corridor of the night.

They were still standing like that, watching, each with his own thoughts, when a quiet voice behind them cut across those thoughts in a chilly way.

"Stand easy, men. Don't make a move . . . none of you."

They froze, knowing at once the identity of that man hidden by the night, knowing his reason for being here, and his full intention.

Out of the eastern shadows came a tall, pale-eyed silhouette, assuming substance and size and outline as he approached. He had a cocked six-gun in his fist. Without a word or a wasted motion, this stranger went among them, throwing their holstered weapons out into the dark. He disarmed every one of them except Dale McAfee. They simply stared at him, then he moved back out again where they could only scarcely make him out.

"All of you but McAfee sit down again," someone snapped.

Rockland's men turned, moving carefully and looking around in the night. They sat, knowing there would be four men hidden there in the darkness. They were not cowed, but they were unarmed—helpless, so they did as they were told and waited.

"McAfee!"

This was a different voice now. It came from west of the little guttering fire and it sounded young, bell-clear, and unmistakably challenging.

McAfee shifted, turning slightly at the waist. "Step up where I can see you!" he called. "You act like a bunch of . . ."

"Shut up!"

That was another new voice. It was a ripped-out, deadly voice, and Dale McAfee, brought up short by it, estimated that this other man was somewhere behind him in a southerly direction.

A slowly pacing man came gradually into sight out of the west. Firelight reached him faintly, showing a smoothness to his face, a rippling youthfulness to his sinewy build, and an unwaveringly solid menace in the way he fixed the Texas Star's foreman with his deeply sunken eyes.

This man said: "McAfee, you're going to get your chance. Don't worry about the others interfering."

"I'm not worrying," McAfee replied, his sharp face getting as tight as wire. "You better be real fast, sonny."

The tall youth said nothing. He had one shoulder down a little, one hand curved at the fingers,and both his knees sprung the slightest bit.

The seated Texas Star men were scarcely breathing. The night air had a sharp scent suddenly, and the vision of every man at this place was inexplicably more acute than it ever normally was.

"You know why, don't you, McAfee?"

"Sure I know. Because that old man got in the way and stopped one accidentally. Hell, I didn't even know him. He just got in the way."

"You could've waited. You could've told him to get clear."

McAfee said nothing. He pushed his feet a little farther apart. He very gently set his stance and curved his body inward at the waist so that his right arm and hand were hanging correctly.

"I guess the old man didn't mean anything to you, McAfee," said the youth. "I guess you figured him for just some old derelict who maybe needed killing."

"No, I didn't figure to kill him," McAfee said, telling the truth. Then he added: "What the hell . . . he was old enough, anyway."

"So are you, McAfee."

McAfee was no coward. He had met no men thus far in his life who could match his craftiness or his gunmanship. He had not the least doubt that the young man over that intervening dark distance from him was no exception to this. What troubled him was the other three, out in the night somewhere, with drawn, cocked guns.

"Maybe I'm old enough to die," McAfee said to Austin King. "But at least I don't need a pack of wolves to back me up when I fight, sonny."

That quiet-toned voice from a northerly direction said: "Rest easy about that, McAfee. We're here just to keep your Texas Star men from joining in with you on the fight."

"And," McAfee stated, speaking a little louder without taking his narrowed gaze off young Austin, "if I down your brother here . . . you're not going to jump me, too?"

"No," Ray King answered from the north of the camp. "Not like you think. But if you kill our

73

brother, why then you'll meet another one of us. And if you kill him, still another of us. You'll die here tonight, McAfee, or you'll meet us one at a time until you do die."

McAfee rocked up in his boots the slightest bit. He said to Austin: "That's fair enough. Maybe that's the way it should be. I didn't mean to kill that old man, but I sure 'nough did kill him. Maybe it's right I got to kill you boys of his one at a time." McAfee paused, breathed deeply in and deeply out, before continuing with: "All right. Any time you're ready, sonny."

That sharp scent in the night became instantly more acute. The Texas Star men sat without breathing. The stars seemed closer, brighter, harder. There was not a sound anywhere.

Austin's right wrist and hand moved in a barely perceptible blur. McAfee was moving, also. One shot rang out, one long dagger of red flame erupted. There was a second shot but it went toward the ground. That second bullet tore up a great gout of sod. Dale McAfee staggered, his knees turned loose, and he went down against the ground with a little rustling sound. He did not move again.

A long mile and a half to the south, where John Rockland was riding beside his daughter, there came upon the late night air a distinct shock wave, a very faint, very distant sound of two nearly simultaneous pistol shots. Rockland yanked his reins back. He tilted his head, listening, then swiftly asked: "What was that?"

Judith's eyes turned black as they widened. She did not answer. She did not have to because they both knew what those faint popping sounds were. They also both guessed what they meant and why.

"Go home," John Rockland said, spinning his horse, hooking the beast savagely with his spurs and lunging away in the direction from which they had just come.

Judy followed him. She ran on down the darkness with a bleakness upon her spirit that made her features ugly and sere and vengeful. She did not race near her father until he slowed within sight of that dying pencil of flame at the holding ground. Then she hauled back to dismount and did not look at her father at all.

Ahead, Texas Star's cowboys were standing silently above a flattened shape upon the earth. They turned as John Rockland came up, stepping out in his longest stride. They moved back a little so that their boss could see. They watched Rockland draw up suddenly and stand there, his face wintery, his eyes ice-like.

"Was it *them?*" Rockland demanded.

The riders nodded. One of them murmured: "They was out there in the night. I reckon they was out there when Miss Judy rode up. They waited. After you rode off, they called McAfee."

"All four of them?"

Ira answered truthfully: "Only one of 'em called out McAfee. The others stood back. Mister Rockland, it was a fair fight."

"Yes," Rockland responded witheringly, "and if one of them hadn't gotten him, the others would have. Where are your guns?"

"Well . . . they got the drop on the lot o' us, Mister Rockland. We wasn't expecting nothing. They come out of the darkness, disarmed us, an' let the young one fight McAfee."

"The young one?"

"Yes, sir. The youngest one of 'em. He was there in town this morning with the others. A sort of hot-eyed-looking young feller, but tall. Tall as the others."

"You mean to say that boy outgunned McAfee?"

"Yes, sir. We all seen it . . . it was fair enough. That boy's got no match with a gun, I tell you that, Mister Rockland."

The owner of Texas Star stood, studying the ground. After several minutes, he said savagely: "We'll see. By God, we'll see if there's no match for that boy. For the lot of them!"

Chapter Seven

Sheriff Bannion went to bed confident that Judy would carry his message to her father, that John Rockland would heed Bannion's good advice, and perhaps, before another day passed, somehow, there would occur to him a way to forestall serious trouble.

He arose the following morning still feeling the same way. He left his room at the hotel, went along to the Shafter Café, got his accustomed seat at the counter—and the sky fell on him.

"I guess old Rockland's fit to be tied over Dale McAfee's killing, isn't he?" the counterman said, making breakfast conversation. "I seen him and his crew ride by a few minutes ago with the body and he looked like a man of thunder for sure."

Bannion got up, turned without a word, and walked out of the café. The counterman looked completely bewildered by this. He scratched his ample belly, scowled, looked down at Bannion's empty place, and waddled away, wagging his head.

Bannion saw the crowd forming down by his jailhouse. He crossed through roadway dust and pushed on through to where John Rockland stood. Texas Star's owner hadn't shaved.

Bannion had never before seen him looking unkempt.

"Go take a look," Rockland said, nodding toward the limp form tied sideways over a saddled horse.

Bannion did not move. "No need," he said. "Come inside."

Rockland tossed his reins to a rider before going after Bannion. "All right," he said to his range men, "take him to the undertaker." He passed into Bannion's office alone, went to a chair, and dropped down. He looked drained dry.

"Bannion," he said, "I want those men caught and held here in jail."

"What are the details?" asked Bannion. "It wasn't a back shot was it?"

Rockland's nostrils flared. He lifted his head until he had to look downward to see the sheriff. "That was a planned killing."

"Most killings are," Bannion murmured, bracing into the wealthy cowman's wrath.

"Premeditated, Bannion. Those men went to my holding ground, called out McAfee, and one of them killed him. The youngest one."

"That would be Austin."

"I want them arrested, tried, and convicted. That was premeditated from start to finish."

"No one would rightly argue about that," said Bannion. "But do any of your men who saw that killing say it was murder?"

John Rockland began to answer, then abruptly checked himself even though he kept staring at Doyle Bannion. He pushed himself out of the chair, saying: "Bannion, are you, or are you not, going to jail those King brothers?"

"If there's a charge, yes. If there is no charge, I can't jail them. That's the law, Mister Rockland."

"Then I'll make the charge. Murder!"

Bannion sat still for a moment. Then he said: "Any witnesses?"

"I'll produce those, too."

Bannion said no more. He tapped his desk. He considered the unreasoning ferocity, the willful hatred in John Rockland's face. He remained silent for several minutes, then finally said: "If anyone's guilty of murder, it's Rufus Paige."

Rockland blinked. He began to scowl. "What are you talking about? Old Rufe wasn't even at the holding ground. He went back to the ranch before sunset for additional supplies."

"Sure," said Bannion. "But that's not the only reason he went back to Texas Star." Bannion got up. "Mister Rockland, I tried hard to prevent this. I think I know where I failed. But that's past and Dale's dead. Now I'm going to make another hard try by telling you *not* to hire any gunfighters."

Rockland glared. "Don't you tell me what to do, Bannion. Damn you, I'll take that badge off you and melt it down into bullets. You remember that. Now, are you going after those Kings or not?"

"I'm going after them," Bannion answered, hardening his gaze against Rockland. "And I'll get them. You have my promise on that. But, Mister Rockland, so help me, if it costs me this badge and a lot more to boot, the day you import gunfighters to Perdition Wells, I'll come after you, too."

Rockland's face darkened. That big vein in the side of his neck swelled. He swung about and rushed from Bannion's office, slamming the door after himself. He called out to his riders: "Head back . . . head for Texas Star! The law's not going to do anything about McAfee, so dammit I am!"

Bannion got to the door in time to see people scatter out of the path of the speeding horsemen as big John Rockland, blindingly mad, led his riders in a rush out of Perdition Wells.

People stared up the roadway after Rockland. When he and his men were out of view, they turned and gazed over where Doyle Bannion was standing with a smoky shading to his eyes, his usually easy-going jaw set like granite. They spoke among themselves and went uneasily about their business. A few, the bolder ones, started for Sheriff Bannion. He saw them coming, brushed right on past, and headed for the livery barn.

"Sam!" he bawled in the stable doorway. "Sam, where are you, consarn it!"

A man appeared through a door at the back of the barn. He stopped and craned a look out at

Sheriff Bannion, squinting. "What's wrong, Doyle?" he asked, beginning to hurry toward the lawman. "What is it?"

"Those four big fellers . . . have they ridden in yet?"

"The King boys? No, I haven't seen them since last night. They rode out of town about a half hour after you did." The liveryman's squint increased until his entire face was pinched up from it. "What's wrong, Doyle? What's goin' on anyway? I just seen Rockland and his crew go bustin' out of town like the devil was after 'em."

"The devil was leading 'em," growled Bannion, and he pushed past Sam and hurried to the stall of his own personal horse. There, he flung on his saddle, bridled and turned the animal. As he mounted, he said: "If anyone but the Kings come looking for me, tell them . . . tell them I'll be back when I get back." He started forward toward the roadway. "And if those damned King brothers are looking for me, Sam, you tell them I'm look-ing for them, too."

Bannion swung his mount northward, eased him over into a slow lope, and kept him at this gait for a full hour. Then, where he cut the tracks of men going toward and returning from Texas Star's holding ground, he turned sharply and began following the tracks leading away from that distant spot. He rode without an awareness of time, or the peculiar coppery glint that came gradually to color this day. It was hot, and this registered in his mind from the steady burning across his shoulders, but the other thing—that peculiar coppery shading to the sun—went unnoticed entirely.

The tracks of four horsemen riding slowly led Bannion out and around Perdition Wells and to a wild plum thicket along a sluggish creek. Here, he saw where the riders had halted a while to smoke a cigarette within sight of town but screened from it. He grunted, thinking: *These Kings sure are careful men.* They had waited to see what would happen in Perdition Wells after McAfee's killing was known there, before riding on in for their personal effects at the hotel. Bannion wondered how far ahead of him they now were? Whether they were still in town, or whether, during his absence tracking them, they had already quietly picked up their bedrolls and ridden on?

He went ahead into town from the south, tied his horse at the jailhouse hitch rack, and crossed through a brassy afternoon to the hotel. As he stepped onto the plank walk, the significance of that strange, metallic lighting struck him and he halted, turned, and put a knowing look at the sun.

There was a sulphur look to the sky, a peculiarly ominous tint of mustard. Not a breath of air stirred anywhere. Bannion was turning, having completed his survey of this phenomenon, when a strolling man passed him with a nod, saying: "Another damned Santa Ana, Sheriff. I guess we'd all best fasten our shutters and wait it out."

Bannion nodded absently and went to the hotel. At the desk, he said to the clerk: "Are the King boys here?" He got an answer that totally surprised him.

"Came in about ten minutes ago, Sheriff. All four of 'em are upstairs in their room."

"Checkin' out, huh?" asked Bannion.

The clerk shook his head, saying: "Not that I know of. Say, Sheriff, about that McAfee killing . . ."

But Bannion was already halfway to the staircase leading up to the guest rooms. He pretended he hadn't heard the clerk's comment and hurried up the steps, without a glance back. He halted on the landing as an angry voice came distinctly to him through a nearby door. Bannion listened, moved closer, and stood to listen some more.

". . . nothing but cold-blooded murderers. I didn't believe there were men like you still left in Texas. Sheriff Bannion told me you weren't gunfighters . . . weren't murderers . . . but now I know better. If I were a man, I'd . . ."

"Lady," came the unmistakable, quiet voice of Ray King, "if you were a man, you wouldn't say one more word."

"No," Judith Rockland shouted at him, her voice

knife-edged with wrath, with deep scorn. "You'd gang up and shoot me, too, wouldn't you? Like animals and cowards kill . . . in a pack!"

"Lady, only one of us faced McAfee. It was a fair fight. We never had any intention it should be anything else."

There was a quick sound of scuffling.

Bannion reached for the knob at exactly the same moment Judith Rockland cried: "Take your hand off me!"

"Lady, you'd best leave now," Bannion heard Ray say. "I was only showing you to the door. You've had your say and you'd better go on home now."

"Yes! So the four of you can ride out of Perdition Wells before my father catches you."

As a different voice responded to Judith, Bannion recognized its cold quality as belonging to Al King. "Miss, if it'll make you feel better, we can wait around for your pappy to come into town. In a way I'd sort of like that, personally. He strikes me as needing a little . . ."

"Never mind, Al," Ray broke in. He sounded tired to Bannion. "Miss Rockland, you go along now . . . please."

The door opened.

Over the head of Judith Rockland, Doyle Bannion and the four King brothers ran their glances together in a moment of stillness.

Then Ray ushered Judith out of the room with

a gentle but firm grasp at her elbow, blocking the opening against Doyle with his bigness.

"You want something, Sheriff?" he asked.

"I want to talk to the four of you," Bannion answered.

"Talk," Hank said harshly from behind Ray. "Go ahead and talk. Only make it short because we're leaving your town for good and all, Sheriff."

"I don't think you're leaving quite yet," Bannion informed the brothers.

At once fiery Austin tried to push around his older brother. Ray stood firm against this pressure, but Austin's voice traveled past his brother. "You want to try and stop us, Sheriff? You'd better have a warrant to do it . . . or you're going to get whittled down to size."

Bannion put out a hand, pushed it against Ray's middle, and stepped forward, saying: "Let me show you boys something."

Ray turned sideways to let Bannion pass, then he faced forward again, exchanging a long, long look with Judith Rockland who remained standing in the empty hallway.

Bannion went to the window and drew back a curtain. He motioned for the brothers to step over and take a look.

Hank and Al came over to stand just behind him.

"Look at that sky," Bannion said, and stepped aside. "Does that mean anything to you west Texas boys?"

Al looked out, then at Bannion without changing expression. Hank, though, looked, then bent to look closer, motioning his youngest brother over to join them.

"A Santa Ana," Hank said. "Hey, Ray, come take a look at this sky."

Ray came, leaving the door ajar. He stood at the window peering out. "Well," he said with solid resignation to his brothers, "I reckon that fixes that. A Santa Ana's sure enough coming."

Al pushed his brother out of the way so he could look out again, saying: "What's a Santa Ana?"

"It's a big wind, Al, like that one we got caught in the night we hit Perdition Wells. You recollect?"

"Recollect!" Al exclaimed. "I'll never forget that wind as long as I live. It liked to peeled the hide off me and my horse both."

"Well, there's another one coming right now."

Austin swore. "Well, hell, then we can't leave," he said, and tossed his hat down as he looked out into the empty hallway. He saw that Judith Rockland was gone. Austin's fists clenched as he announced: "Now we'll get into it for sure! That girl's gone, and, sure as hell is afire, she'll tell her paw we're stuck here until the Santa Ana passes."

Chapter Eight

There was no warning when the Santa Ana struck, which was unusual. Ordinarily that furnace-hot stinging wind up out of Mexico came gradually, turning the sky dark, whipping sand in off the desert with a force that made each grain seem as sharp-honed as a knife blade. It turned the sky dun-saffron and made the sun seem glazed with a deathly mustard-like hue, but ordinarily none of these things happened until that warning stillness, that peculiar coppery shade, filled the day.

But this time the wind came with tornado-like force out of the distant south with a shrieking howl and a gale-like mad whirling. It struck Perdition Wells, making buildings quiver on their foundations, slamming doors and shutters until those sounds rose over the wind's keening howl like cannon fire.

Another distinctive thing about a Santa Ana wind was the metallic scent that filled the air. It was a smell like the dust from opened, dry graves—musty, bitter, and encompassing. It did no good to close windows against this odor because it permeated everything. It filled that room at the Perdition Wells Hotel where five men stood looking at one another while around them the world turned prematurely dark and sulphur-glazed, while the building shuddered where it stood, and while the rising scream rose fiercely around them.

"A bad one!" Bannion shouted, and Ray King nodded.

"Never saw one come so quickly before!"

Bannion went to the door, paused there to look back, saw how those four big men were standing, still gazing from that bizarre mustard-light beyond the window to one another. He knew the Kings would not leave town now.

Bannion went down to the lobby. People in off the sidewalk were huddling there, talking excitedly, and beating dust from their clothing.

A gaunt man walked up to Bannion, bent forward, and shouted to him over the howl of wind: "Don't like this, Doyle! Town never had a chance! It blew us right in off the walkway! Never saw one hit like this before! Think there'll be casualties . . . men caught in their fields . . . !"

Bannion nodded without making any attempt to shout back. He went as far as the doorway and braced into the power of the storm, making a quick survey of the roadway. There was nothing in sight, no people, no horses at the tie racks. He could hardly make out the opposite buildings. Tan dust was everywhere. It seeped in around windows to make small piles. It clogged a man's nostrils in a matter of seconds.

Bannion returned to the center of the room, everything but this very real peril pushed aside in his thoughts. He had been through his share of Santa Anas. There was an invariable sequence to be followed. He did not relish this duty, but then he had never relished it. Still, he had to go out there, go up and down the sidewalks making sure there was nothing left outside by merchants that could become a projectile. He also had to make sure there was no one caught out in the wind who might need help—women or children or old people. This sometimes happened, but not often. At least not among long-time residents of Milam County, anyway, because after one or two such experiences, even children understood the ominous warning when the sky turned that coppery color.

However, he had had no warning this time, and therefore his windbreaker was hanging over at the jailhouse. A person did not wear a windbreaker for warmth—the Santa Ana winds were never cold—he wore it for protection. A man, lightly clothed, going out into that raging hell could actually have his skin pitted until it bled profusely in five minutes of excruciating torture, when he was subject to that howling, sandblasting force.

There was another danger, too. If caught away from anything to grab hold of, many a person had been lifted up, flung down, and swept along with broken arms, legs, or ribs. People were not commonly killed by a Santa Ana, unless struck by some flying object, but it had happened.

Bannion went to the clerk and asked for a coat. The milling men and women over at the counter, ganged together like bewildered sheep, watched Bannion shrug into an over-size garment that the clerk produced. They stood dumb, knowing Bannion must go out, yet wishing to say something, even if only to warn him, to suggest that he wait a bit, to give some kind of an opinion. None of them, though, said anything.

Bannion knotted a handkerchief over his face, drew it up under his eyes, yanked his hat down until only a meager line showed up across his eyes, then he started to the door. He was reaching for the knob with both hands, ready to fight the force that would tear into the room the second he drew that panel inward, when a big hand closed down over his forearm. Bannion turned with annoyance, anticipating some remonstrance from a well-wisher. What he saw was the four big men from west Texas. Each of them had on a windbreaker and a mask such as the one Bannion wore.

It was the eldest man's hand upon Bannion's arm. Ray King let go, pulled down his handkerchief, put his head close to Bannion's ear, and said: "Two of us will take this side of the road. The other two will take the yonder side. We know what to do. You do whatever else has got to be done, and we'll meet you at the jailhouse."

Bannion squinted into that rugged face with its smooth layers of suntan, and nodded. Several things he might have said came to mind, but he said none of them. He waited until Ray King had his mask up again, then reached for the door. As soon as the latch was released a terrific force struck the door, nearly wrenching it away from Bannion's grasp. He gestured the four big men out, then turned, holding stubbornly to the door, and fought it closed.

The wind whooped down upon these five crouching figures. It pummeled them, pried in under their masks and hat brims, and stung with the force of a thousand tiny fists. It beat steadily against the full length of their bodies and within seconds it made breathing difficult.

Ray put a hand upon Al's arm to detain him. He then made an onward motion to young Austin and Hank. These two went forward at once, fought their way halfway out across the road, then had to join arms in a locked manner and literally fight for each forward step. Here, where no obstruction minimized the wind's full fury, only the strongest men could remain upright, and, in fact, except that Austin and Hank were holding mightily to one another, even those two, young and strong as they were, would never have made it.

When they did though, and paused to encircle an upright upon the far plank walk, fighting for breath, to Bannion, Ray, and Al, they could be seen only dimly.

Ray tapped Bannion, made a gesture indicating he and Al would start patrolling, then took his brother and started off. Bannion watched them fade out, then he turned north and, by hugging storefronts, got to the general store. This had been his initial destination because the proprietor always had a large display of goods outside his big front window, and in times past people had been badly bruised by flying pitchforks, rakes, even corrugated washboards.

What he found though, after getting inside and kicking past the hastily flung-down objects that had been frantically hurled inside from the plank walk, was that a length of trace chain had whipped upward and broken the front window.

The storekeeper and his one clerk were desperately struggling to fit a large board over the opening. Both men were bleeding from slivers of hurled window glass. Neither of them had a coat on, and they were fast weakening under the massive onslaughts of that outside fury.

Bannion climbed up to throw his shoulder against the board. He felt it go forward a little. Then it was struck by two additional shoulders and went nearly into place. Bannion yelled something. Neither the storekeeper nor his clerk heard this because wind whipped the words away almost before they were spoken, but that third strong presence heartened the store men and even without hearing Bannion's profane encouragement they fought, gasping, to press that board in close enough.

At once both store men began to drive nails furiously. Bannion slanted an upward narrowed look, saw the nail heads glistening, and very gingerly withdrew his shoulder. The plank quivered and vibrated, but it held.

The clerk stepped away from the window into three inches of gritty sand, turned to look upward where his employer was finishing pounding in the last nail, and fainted. Bannion grasped the man's bloody shirt, dragged him behind a counter, and bent over him, ascertaining that it was nothing more than a faint.

When he rose up, the merchant was panting there with both arms braced. He gasped: "Is he bad hurt?" Bannion shook his head. The merchant twisted to frown downward. "Fainted?" Again Bannion nodded. The storekeeper said: "I'll fetch him some whiskey."

Bannion left the store, was rushed along for a hundred feet, bumping and turning until he caught hold of a railing, and there he halted, looking beyond the last building out across the rangeland. Everything five feet beyond was utterly blotted out by that mustard-tan gritty blight. He stood for a moment with his back against the wind, breathing deeply, then he turned, dropped his head, and began fighting his way southward a foot at a time directly into the face of this unrestrained natural force.

Somewhere west of town there was a loud report, then the grinding crash of a roof being torn away and flung violently against another building. This was the only sound Bannion could distinguish over the howl, the shriek of this worst of all Santa Anas he'd ever experienced.

He could progress southward only about fifty feet at a time without having to halt, turn his back, lean against that tangible force, and struggle for more of the insufficient air before attempting to go farther. Once, something struck his lower legs. He bent down, caught hold of something furry, lifted it close enough to see it, and saw a terrified little mongrel dog writhing in his grip. He crushed this small animal against his chest and backed along the plank walk to the first door-way. There, he flung the panel open, dropped the little dog inside, and slammed the door closed. This took more of Bannion's energy. He hung there in that recessed place, panting.

It was then that he heard something that might have been a door slamming or a rooftree snapping, or even a piece of tin being whipped away in the wind. But what he thought was that this sharp popping sound was a gunshot.

He left the doorway and went onward again, bearing southward, body bent nearly double, one arm flung out to feel the wood siding on his left, and in this manner got back to the hotel. Here, he could make out blurred movement dead ahead through the grating wetness of his slitted eyes. He kept on, passing the hotel door, and closed his fingers over a man's upper arm.

It was Al King. With Al was Ray. Al tugged at Sheriff Bannion's arm and turned back, going southward a hundred yards, following Ray. The three of them got into a doorway with wind tearing at them but with its greater force whipping past. Al pushed his mouth against Bannion's temple and shouted.

"Someone . . . over at . . . jailhouse . . . fired a gun. You hear it?"

Bannion nodded, although he had no idea where that earlier sound had come from, nor, for that matter, that it was actually a gunshot.

Al pushed in close again. "Ray says . . . let's go over there."

Bannion nodded a second time. He pushed out of the doorway, got to the plank walk's very edge, and hung to an upright, steadying himself. Now, the dust was so bad he could not make out even the opposite side of the road.

Ray King came up. He and Al had their arms locked together at the elbow. Ray pushed Bannion roughly away from the post, rammed a powerful arm through Bannion's arm, hooked it hard, and dragged Bannion down into the roadway.

Al's legs went out from under him as though struck by a log. Ray and Bannion set themselves against this dragging force. Al managed somehow to get up and the three of them forged ahead. They could not determine the plank walk when it loomed close and this time Bannion stumbled and the other two braced hard until he could regain his balance. In this fashion they lurched to the left, sometimes gaining, sometimes losing, headway, but endlessly struggling until they arrived in front of the jailhouse. Here, Bannion saw without really noticing it that his horse, left tied earlier at the rack, was no longer there.

Bannion lurched for the door, felt for the latch, lifted it, and nearly fell into the room beyond. Al did fall. He stumbled against his brother, went down on all fours. Then, when the door slammed behind them effectively closing out the threshing wind, Al made a heavy effort to regain his feet. Ray caught his right arm, giving a rough assist.

Bannion's jailhouse was solid adobe. It was a very old building, having once been a Mexican barracks, and after Mexico lost Texas, it had then been a Texas Ranger post. With walls of adobe mud three feet thick it was the only building still in use at Perdition Wells as an office. It was also the only building in town that was literally soundproof, and therefore, while the raging storm outside could be faintly heard, the loud, dry coughing of someone within the office sounded much louder.

Bannion yanked down his mask, threw aside his hat, and looked over where Hank King was trying to stifle his coughing with dippers full of water from the drinking bucket. Young Austin had his hat off. His hair stood out in every direction, stiff with static electricity. His eyes were fast swelling and badly bloodshot. Ray and Al shucked their windbreakers, and all five of them stood there looking dumbly at one another, sucking this relatively clean air deep down.

"Damn," husked Al, groping his way to a bench. "I can hardly see."

Bannion cautioned: "Don't rub your eyes. Go get some water at the bucket, soak a rag with it, and wash them real gently." His own eyes grated in their sockets. "You rub your eyes now and the sand'll rupture blood vessels. You'll be blind for a while. Be careful even when you wash them."

Ray King coughed and spat and coughed again. He found a chair, dropped down into it, and threw back his head. Exhaustion was deeply etched into every line of his sprawling, big body. After a while he said: "The worst one I ever saw. It's like a genuine hurricane."

"How do you know it isn't?" asked Austin. "I don't see how this town stands that abuse."

"Some of it didn't," replied Hank. "I heard a roof tear off somewhere west of town."

Ray brought his head forward and down. He looked at those badly punished men. "Who fired that shot?" he asked.

Austin said: "I did."

Each face turned to regard the youth. No one spoke.

Austin ran a hand through his awry hair. He went to Bannion's desk and perched upon it. He looked at them all, but he looked longest at Ray.

"Hank and I went to the livery barn," Austin said. "Everything there was in pretty good shape, only . . ."

"Yes?" Al urged, sounding irritable.

"The liveryman told us that Rockland girl left town about five minutes before the storm struck."

Even cold-blooded Al King lifted his head to regard Austin now. All four of the men sat there looking at Austin, the youngest King brother, struck dumb by their instant realization of what his words meant.

Chapter Nine

Hank had his coughing under control now. He looked at Bannion, saying: "Any chance, Sheriff . . . any chance she might've got under cover somewhere?"

Bannion had instantly considered this after Austin had said what he'd learned at the livery barn. Now he shook his head. "There's nothing between here and Texas Star except some little arroyos and a few trees. No buildings she could hole up in, and that's what it takes for a person to ride out one of these storms . . . four good walls and a solid roof."

Ray King drew his legs under him. He leaned forward in the chair, looking straight ahead at nothing. "She'd get lost," he said quietly. "No matter how good a homing instinct her horse had, it wouldn't work in a storm as bad as this one."

Bannion shared this belief. He said to Austin: "Why didn't that damned fool at the barn keep her there?"

Austin looked at Bannion and shrugged. "I reckon he had no idea, like the rest of us, it would strike this fast and hard. At any rate he didn't, and that's what counts now."

"Yeah," Ray murmured so quietly they scarcely

heard him. "That's what counts now." He straightened back in the chair, looking over at Bannion. When he spoke again, it was in the same quiet way, as though he were actually thinking aloud. "A man couldn't go after her on horseback . . . he'd have to go afoot."

"If he went at all," said Hank, from over by the water bucket. "That's a pretty big country out there, Ray."

Bannion took off the coat the hotel clerk had given him. He tossed it aside and got his own windbreaker from a wall peg, put it on, and sat back down while he beat dust from his hat and his handkerchief that he had used as a mask. As though instructing children and without once looking up at them, Bannion said to the west Texans: "You take four lariats. You stretch them to their maximum limits and each man ties an end of one around his wrist. Then you fan out. If the lariats are sixty-footers, you can cover a heap of ground. Then you keep walking."

Hank finished bathing his face and made room for Al. Young Austin sat on Bannion's desk, looking steadily at the sheriff. Ray removed his hat, savagely beat it against one leg, then crushed it back onto his head.

"You got the lariats?" he asked.

Bannion bobbed his head up and down, retied the handkerchief over his face, and got up. He went to a closet and returned with several coiled hard-twist ropes. He gave Ray one, Austin one, Al one, Hank one, and kept the fifth one for himself. "You really only need four," he explained to Hank, who was regarding him with a little scowl. "But when you find the person you're after, why then you tie him . . . or her . . . with the fifth one, so he . . . she . . . don't get blown away again."

Bannion stood there watching Al at the water bucket gingerly bathing his eyes. "Maybe only a couple of us could do it," he said.

Ray stood up to his full towering height and looked at Al exactly as Bannion was doing. "Hell, Sheriff, a little sand in the face wouldn't stop my brothers. How about that, Al?"

From the water bucket there came a soft cursing, then, as Al raised his face and lowered the wet rag, he growled: "A little sand wouldn't, no . . . but a damned world filled with sand might. Just you be dog-goned sure my end of the rope is tied tight. I got a hunch I'll be blind ten minutes after we walk out of here."

Ray said to Bannion: "You take the easterly end of the line and we'll be guided by your pulls."

"I intended to. Now remember this . . . one hard yank means stop. Two hard yanks means go ahead. Three means bear west, and four means bear east. That's all you've got to remember. If something happens to one of you, sit down. We'll all feel the drag and converge toward it."

"What could happen?" queried Austin.

"Probably nothing," Bannion responded. "But one time I was on a rope posse, such as this, when a loose horse ran between two of us. I was laid up for two months with a dislocated shoulder." Then he smiled at young Austin, went to the door, and said: "If you're ready, we'd better get started. If she's down, the sand could cover her over completely in ten minutes."

Al left the water bucket with some hard words, got into his windbreaker, and started to tie his wet neckerchief over his face.

Bannion said: "Use a dry one. Dust'll clog that one so you can't breathe in two minutes." Al looked unhappy as he complied.

They grouped around Bannion at the door, towering above him. He looked into their faces and passed each of them the end of a lariat. Without speaking he made his end of a lariat secure to his wrist. Also without saying anything, the others did likewise.

Then Ray King put a considering gaze upon Bannion. "I kind of had you sized up for a pretty good man," he said. "I guess that other thing . . ."— and they all knew he meant the killing of Dale McAfee—"maybe prevents us from being friends, though."

Al King's dark and swollen eyes held to Bannion from the thin slit between hat brim and mask. Bannion regarded Al in long silence; he was the only one of these four men he had an aversion to. Al, understanding this, said in a grumbly and muffled way: "Well, hell, I don't like you, either."

Young Austin laughed aloud, and Hank, standing next to Austin, chuckled deep in his chest.

All Bannion said was: "We'll let the wind take us beyond town, then I'll lead off easterly a ways before we start north. I know the direction she would have taken. You fellers be guided by my rope. The main thing is to keep up, and keep at the end of your ropes. Don't let a lot of slack build up." He paused, looked at them, lifted his shoulders, and let them fall. "I have no idea how far we'll have to go or how long this will take. I only know we've got to make the effort."

"Sure," Ray said softly. "We understand."

Bannion turned, took a firm hold of the door, and opened it. At once all that screaming tumult that had been muted by the jailhouse walls roared around them. They crowded outside, waited until Bannion closed the door after them, then went scudding into the roadway.

At once the raging wind engulfed them. It was worse than before. They could barely make out the man on each side of them. They let it almost carry them to the north end of town, then Bannion began paying out rope and working his way off to the right. The others, guided by their ropes, drifted along with him until, from one end to the other end, they were strung out over a hundred-and-eighty-foot line. Now, none of them could see the other. Only that whipping hard-twist rope linked them. Along it was transferred the only contact they had. It became a kind of hemp telegraph. Bannion signaled for them to drift still farther eastward, and they responded at once.

Bannion, experienced in this savage contest of man against Nature, let the wind do most of the work. He moved his legs mechanically, taking small steps, compelling the storm to push him along. In this fashion he hoarded his energy. Once, when a fractional lull came, he sighted Ray King downcountry on his left. The oldest King brother was doing as Bannion was himself doing—making the wind work for him. Then that lull passed, the wild force returned, and Bannion was fiercely pummeled.

None of them could see ten feet ahead. For Bannion this required total reliance upon instinct. But he was neither a novice at what he was about, nor likely to be misled from his sense of direction. What he feared was not that they wouldn't find Judith Rockland, but that they might, if she was down, pass over her. This had happened in the past when rope posses were searching blindly for lost people during a Santa Ana.

Bannion had the fourth lariat around his middle. Once, a loop of it slipped down nearly tripping him. He fixed the loop, went another hundred yards, and felt a sharp tug on his guide line. He did not converge, but waited, and, true to his guess, Ray had only stumbled. Within seconds the signal came to advance, and Bannion went on again.

It was useless to try and detect foreign sounds. The wind's howling fury drowned out everything else. It cut around and lashed their faces, their eyes, but it was not as bad in this respect, Bannion knew, with their backs to it, as it would be later, when they had to face its unbridled fury on the return trip. He wondered briefly about Al King's eyes, then a frantic tugging came on his wrist from Ray. He did not know whether this signal originated with Ray or was being transmitted from farther along the rope, but his heart struck hard in its cage, bringing hope flashing upward.

Bannion halted. The frantic, insistent tugging continued. Then a violent jerk wrenched Bannion off balance, drawing him fiercely westward. He turned a little, trying to keep pace with that hard pulling. Now the wind beat mercilessly along his side driving him relentlessly ahead, around, and partially away from Ray. He fought for balance and footage. He kept his mouth open, his head bent, and one shoulder up to protect his eyes as much as possible, and came finally toward something crouched and lumpy in the mad-whirling sand and dust, low upon the ground. He very dimly made out other converging man shapes staggering like scarecrows inward from the west.

Ray caught Bannion's trouser leg and yanked hard. Bannion fought down to his knees and finally saw the sifted-over lumpiness Ray King was striving to shield with his body.

They had found her!

Ray was already working a handkerchief over Judith's face. He had brushed most of the sand off her upper body, her face and head. Bannion at once made loose that fourth lariat, tied one end to the unconscious girl's gritty wrist, and made the other end fast to his free arm. Young Austin worked his way in close and the five of them made a barrier of their bodies around the girl. Al fashioned a spare cloth over her hair and upper face. Ray leaned, worked both arms through the sand, got a good grip, and strained. The others instantly rose up with their powerful arms helping him stand upright.

Bannion now took charge. By hand motions and by pushing and pulling, he got Austin and Al ahead of Ray in a manner that would break the force of the wind's direct beating. They understood his purpose, and when all of them began struggling back toward Perdition Wells, Ray had a meager amount of help in his struggling onward battle into the face of the storm.

Bannion remained with Ray, partially supporting the larger man with his arm. It was a staggering procession, at times forced off course, at other times made to stand nearly motionless while leaning far forward into the undiminishing power of the Santa Ana's fiercest onslaughts.

Bannion twice had to correct the direction of Austin and Al, because the wind made them reel easterly. Both times, benumbed, they failed to make a good enough correction afterward.

Then Ray began to lose ground, to weave unsteadily. He finally went down, struggling to the very last but overcome by exhaustion, and came to rest, still hugging Judith to him, upon his knees. Bannion instantly yanked on their ropes fetching back Austin and Al. The four of them crowded up close to give Ray and the unconscious girl what protection they could.

Al would have taken Judith when they started out again, but Ray would not release her to him. He and Austin went ahead and this time Hank joined Bannion, one on each side of Ray, bolstering him onward. When a sudden momentary hush came, once, Bannion distinctly heard the sobbing gasp of Ray King's labored breathing. Then that second passed and Bannion had to fight ahead, correct their position again, and drop back to resume his station beside the staggering oldest King brother.

There was no sensation of time passing. It might have been still the morning of this frightful day, except that in each man the knowledge lay solidly that this day had to be nearly spent. To Bannion this meant that the Santa Ana must begin to subside, for rarely did these wild storms last longer than one day. About this one, though, he could only speculate; it was following precedent only in a loosely general way.

He was unconsciously straining to hear the coming of a lull, which generally began near the end of a Santa Ana. They came, gustily and infrequently at first, then, later, they came more often until, for whole minutes at a time, there would be nothing at all but the distant scream of high wind passing overhead.

None came now though, and after a time, when Bannion was sure they had reached Perdition Wells again, he forgot to listen for them.

They had missed the main roadway entirely and came down into a back alleyway where Bannion had to halt them long enough to get his bearings, before he could lead them onward again, replacing Al who went back to join Hank in supporting Ray. This alleyway was fortunately the one that led due south to the rear of Bannion's jailhouse. It offered protection east and west, but none whatsoever north and south, which was the way of the wild wind, and in fact, because that unfettered howling pressure was compressed here, it made the last hundred yards the most punishing of all.

Bannion got ahead, crashed open the rear door

of his building, and guided them one by one inside as they materialized out of the dust. Hank, the last one in, stumbled over their dragging lariats and fell heavily half in, half out of the doorway. He tried to rise up but dissolved loosely back down again. Bannion tore off his face mask, yelled at Austin to help him, and between them they got Hank inside and the door forced closed and barred.

At once an incredible silence engulfed them, its only disturbing sound the rattling, hacking breathing of men who sank down wherever they stopped, and lay like stone.

Chapter Ten

Bannion lit a lamp, removed his hat and wind-breaker, and went over where Ray King sat in a half-dead posture, still holding Judith Rockland. He took the girl in both arms to a strap-steel cell and put her tenderly upon a bunk there.

He next got water and washed her face, forced a trickle down her throat, and unbuttoned her jacket. He then left a soaked rag over her forehead and went after a long, cold drink of water for himself.

Austin King sat up from where he'd dropped, along with his brothers, upon the jailhouse floor. He probed his eyes very gingerly, rose up, and groped to the water bucket to begin that gentle bathing that eased the pure agony almost at once.

When he looked around and saw Bannion loosening the coats of his brothers, he said: "Damned if you aren't the toughest little man I ever saw, Sheriff."

Bannion twisted from the waist. "Size only means you make a good target and it takes more food to fill you up." He resumed his work and rose when Hank and Al and Ray were divested of hats, masks, and coats. "Give them each a dipper of water," he ordered.

Time ran on. In the near silence of the jailhouse

the outside raging storm continued to tear at Perdition Wells and its furious howl sounded very distant, very muted.

Hank coughed and retched and jack-knifed his legs. There was red froth at his lips.

Ray was nearly an hour before moving. Meanwhile young Austin and Doyle Bannion worked over Judith and the others. Austin, possessing the resiliency of youth, shook off the terror and suffering of that ordeal much sooner than did his older brothers.

Once, watching Bannion as he gently worked over the girl, he said: "One thing I'd like to know. Why do they call this kind of a storm a Santa Ana?"

"Santa Anna," explained Bannion, "was a great Mexican general. He was the fellow who led the attack on our Alamo. He was also the president and dictator of Mexico. But that's not why this kind of a wind was named after him. In the early days, when Texans revolted against Mexico, Santa Anna came marching north up out of Mexico with an enormous army. Folks said you could see the dust that army raised for fifty miles. Ever since then these terrific dust storms have been called Santa Anas."

"How long do they last?"

"¿Quién sabe?" muttered Bannion, watching dark color come into Judith's cheeks. "Who knows? Usually about a day . . . sometimes maybe two days. I wouldn't make any guesses about

111

this one. It's not following the usual pattern, at all. Fetch me a dipper of water, would you?"

Austin got the water, watched Bannion hold the girl's head up while she drank, then he turned when Al groaned, and went over to his brother. A moment later Bannion appeared, putting on his windbreaker. Austin looked up quickly.

"Now what?" he asked.

"We need a doctor here. I'm going for him." Bannion nodded toward Al King. "His eyes are in damned poor shape. He shouldn't have come with us."

Al's lips parted. "Damn you," he rasped at Bannion. "If I could stand up . . . if I could see you . . . damned if I wouldn't bust you in the snoot."

"What for?"

"For being so healthy, that's what for."

Bannion grinned.

Austin grinned back. "I'll wash him while you're gone," the youth said, "unless you need me with you."

"No. You watch 'em. This won't take long."

Bannion went back out into the roadway. His old enemy was waiting. It struck him a savage blow, carrying him along in its shrieking grip until he managed to reach for the woodwork of a recessed doorway. There, he got in safely and banged with a balled fist until someone inside opened the door, leaned against it to keep it from being flung back, and poked a screwed-up face forward.

Bannion recognized what of this leathery countenance he could see and shouted over the wind: "Come with me, Doc! I got some folks for you to look at up at the jailhouse."

The man behind that door said something fierce and scalding, closed the door, and reappeared moments later wrapped in a ragged old Army greatcoat and a shapeless old forage cap. He and Bannion locked arms and began the return trip. They got to the jailhouse and pushed their way inside.

There, the grizzled old medical man flapped dust from his coat and glowered around him.

From the floor where he was sitting, holding a bloody handkerchief to his mouth, Hank King said: "A damned Yankee." He was referring to the doctor's Union Army blue greatcoat and his forage cap.

The medical man whirled, put an iron-like look downward, and spoke right back. "If you don't want Yankee help, you can damned well cough your guts out for all I care!"

Austin, helping Al sit up, swung his head around.

Bannion seized the doctor's arm and hustled him into the little cell where Judith Rockland lay, unevenly breathing and with a strange, unnatural pinkness to her cheeks.

The doctor halted dead still. "Why . . . this is Judy Rockland," he said, sounding aghast.

"She tried to ride home," explained Bannion. "The storm caught her and we went searching for her. How does she look, Doc?"

The medical man flung aside his cap, shook out of his coat, and went toward the bunk. "Go on," he ordered Sheriff Bannion. "Go on out of here. Go nurse those smart-talking Rebel whelps out there. I'll take care of Miss Judy."

Bannion left the cell.

Austin had Al up and was guiding the nearly blind man over to the water bucket. He shot Bannion a look. It was dark and menacing.

Bannion matched his look right back at him.

"Son, that war is long over now. An aftermath of it is what's caused all this today and yesterday. That doctor in there, it just so happens, worked on about as many Confederates as Yanks. He saved lives for four years without caring which side they belonged to. And in case you're interested . . . he's only got one lung to show for all the suffering he endured, too."

Austin's hard look began to fade, but he said caustically: "He's mighty sharp with his tongue, Sheriff."

Bannion nodded. "Around here we put up with it. You see, we figure being in pain a lot of the time like he is, that's his privilege."

Austin moved closer to the bucket with Al. He

reached for a wet rag, and Al, his face inflamed and badly swollen, said through locked teeth: "You leave that doctor alone, Austin. Now give me a wet rag."

Bannion had a half-empty bottle of confiscated whiskey in his desk. He got this, poured out a double shot of it, and made Ray drink it. He then gave another drink to Hank, and helped him up onto a bench where the ill man immediately stretched out his full length and went limp all over. He breathed with difficulty and kept the red-flecked handkerchief to his lips.

Ray came back to full awareness very gradually. He was the most used up of them all and his face was putty-gray except around the eyes. There, he was as swollen- and damaged-looking as the others. He watched Bannion move among them for a time, then he levered himself upright, got to his feet, and wobbled there as a great oak weaves in a high wind.

"No need to move," Bannion advised. "Just sit down and rest. The doctor'll get to each and every one of us after a bit."

"Sheriff?"

Bannion went over beside Ray. "Yes?"

"How was she?"

"The doc's with her now. I think she'll be all right. She's got a lot of sand inside her, but she's conscious and she's breathing."

Ray sat down upon a chair, covered his eyes

with both hands, and said: "Austin? Austin, where are you?"

"Over here. What do you want?"

"Some water on a rag."

Bannion got it for Ray and took it back to him. He helped the eldest of the Kings to rid himself of the residue of grit and sand, and, after that, to bathe his blood-red anguished eyes gingerly.

The doctor came out into Bannion's office, looked bleakly at the battered and broken men, and blew out a big breath. "Tough Texans," he growled, passing over to Hank. He stood over him, looking down. "Why, hell . . . your pappy would be ashamed of you." He put forth a rough hand, yanked away Hank's lip covering, and bent over. "Mica!" he exclaimed. "Mica's in your lungs, boy. Try not to take any real deep breaths." He straightened, and turned his gaze toward Ray. "You'll be fine in a couple of weeks," he said to Hank. "Just avoid all exertion, and make sure you eat plenty, and rest. Get lots of rest."

He pulled Ray's hands away from his face, squinted, and as he studied the eldest King's eyes said to Bannion: "Sheriff, you got any boric acid in this rat hole you call a jailhouse?"

Bannion said he had a bottle of it in his gun cabinet.

The doctor drew upright, frowning. "It won't do your guns any good, dammit. Go fix this man a big cup full of the stuff and have him bathe his eyes one at a time until the foreign particles wash out of them."

The doctor then moved over to where Austin and Al were standing at the water bucket. He viewed Al for a silent moment, then he said: "Same thing for you. Boric acid. Don't rub your eyes . . . any of you. I know they itch, but I don't give a damn. Just don't rub them, unless, of course, you'd like to have impaired vision the rest of your lives."

Then he turned his attention to young Austin, teetered up and down on his heels as he considered him. "Nothing wrong with you," he said. "Probably had sense enough to keep your back to the wind."

Austin stood there steadily, regarding the old doctor, his face smoothed-out and his manner restrained.

"You remind me of someone," the doctor said, his tone changing. "Someone I once picked a musket ball out of. A Rebel officer. You're the spitting image of him, boy . . . except that he didn't have to get that tough look on his face because he *was* tough."

Bannion looked over at the youngest King, saw Austin's lips flatten, his eyes flash quick points of fire. Then the old doctor was speaking again, apparently entirely unimpressed by the warning he could not avoid seeing in Austin's eyes. He now had both hands clasped behind his back as he teetered up and down.

"You're too young and probably too scatter-brained to ever have heard of this Rebel officer, sonny, but all the same you're a dead ringer for him."

Austin stepped clear of Al. He was white from throat to eyes.

Bannion got up swiftly, ready to lunge between those two. But the old medical man stood firm, speaking again, his faded old eyes utterly fearless in the face of Austin's menacing stare.

"That Rebel officer's name was Alpheus King, sonny. Ah, but that was another time, sonny, another age. They made *real* men in those times . . . not would-be men." The doctor began to turn away, still with his hands clasped behind his back.

From in front of the water bucket Al, in that ripped-out way he had of speaking, said: "Austin, leave that man alone."

A solid hush filled the office.

Over on the bench Hank King used both hands to push himself upright. In his chair Ray King lifted his head, put his bloodshot stare straight ahead, and Bannion said, later, that despite the storm you could have heard a pin drop in his office.

The doctor strode over to Bannion and stopped. "Miss Judith will need a lot of care. She's got the fever that goes with sand sickness, Doyle. When her paw comes for her, you tell him not to try and take her out to the ranch. She should be put to bed over at the hotel and kept there for at least a month. If she's subjected to any draught or is allowed to have a visitor with a chest cold . . . and she catches the thing . . . she's likely to die. You tell John Rockland that. And you tell him, if he doesn't like hearing that from you, to come see me and I'll tell him enough to curl his damned ears."

Bannion walked to the door with the doctor. Behind them four sets of inflamed but very steady eyes followed the old man. Bannion helped the old man into his greatcoat and handed him his old forage cap.

The doctor turned, ran his brittle stare over those watching men, and said: "Every man is actually two men. I'm no exception. I'm a doctor first, and just like anyone else when I'm not doctoring. Of course I know who you are. I'd have to be deaf and blind not to have heard all that's been said since you rode into this town. Well, let me tell you one thing . . . I knew your father during the war. I also knew him here. I recognized him the same week he drifted into town. You don't dig in a man's guts without remembering certain things about him. Your pappy used to sit out the summer evenings with me on my back porch, drinking a little, smoking a little, and talking about the things that used to be." He shot a look over at Austin. "You favor him most, boy, except for one thing. Just like I told you, your paw was a real man. He didn't have to look tough ever . . . he *was* tough."

There was a long silence. The old man sighed, put out a hand to the door latch, and spoke again, more softly this time, and with his wintry gaze softening, too.

"You boys come and see me when you're fit and able. I want to tell you something the colonel told me about the lot of you one time." Then the doctor lifted the latch, held that quivering panel, and concluded with: "You're wondering why I, a Yankee, didn't turn your father in for the reward. I'll tell you why. Because he was worth a hundred of the kind of men who were seeking him, and I've always held manhood supreme . . . Rebel or Yankee manhood. When you're a doctor, you do silly things like that because ideals don't mean as much to you as the great men, big and little, who sometimes have to die for ideals."

Bannion went out with him into the storm and guided the doctor back to his residence. Afterward, he stood a moment, alone and quiet with his private thoughts, in the doctor's doorway, before fighting his way back to the jailhouse.

Chapter Eleven

Bannion got Judith moved to the hotel the following morning. The Santa Ana was beginning to fade out in a gusty way. He also guided the King brothers to their room and helped them bathe and bed down. After that Bannion soaked his own carcass for a solid hour in a hot bath, then fell into bed and slept like a log until late in the afternoon.

When he arose, the wind had turned to a whipping, stinging freshet, still strong enough to make people bend into it, but without that ground force that had earlier filled it with sand and mustard-colored dust.

Perdition Wells began to come out, to take stock, to shovel and sweep out. At the general store they measured a piece of glass and cut it, but they could not yet install it. Nor would they until the wind died entirely.

The wind, being higher from earth now, was cleaner. It was also pleasantly cool. The overhead sky, though, retained its coppery hue. When the sun sank this second day of the storm, it was a murky, diluted red.

Bannion, in fresh clothing and wearing a lighter coat, made his rounds of town. His eyes were still bloodshot, they still grated in their sockets, but nearly all the pain was gone from them. He heard from two score residents about the damage they had incurred. He also heard profane pronouncements concerning this particular Santa Ana.

At sunset, he visited Judith Rockland in her hotel room. The old doctor was with her. He was sitting comfortably upon a leather sofa, smoking a vile pipe and quietly talking. Judith was sitting up. She still had that unnatural flush to her cheeks but her eyes were almost clear.

She smiled at Sheriff Bannion, saying: "The doctor told me how you and those . . . those King men, found me and brought me back to town at the height of the storm. Sheriff, I'm very grateful to you."

"Not to me," Bannion said, removing his hat, dropping down upon the same sofa with the doctor. "All I did was show those big west Texans how we hunt for folks during a Santa Ana. That eldest one . . . his name is Ray . . . he picked you up and carried you all the way back here, straight into the teeth of that storm. It's him you owe your gratitude to, Miss Judy."

The girl's smile dwindled. She kept looking at Bannion, but said nothing at all.

The doctor watched these two, then cleared his throat and stood up. "I'll go along and look at our Rebel cubs," he muttered.

Bannion said: "Doc, go easy on that Rebel talk, will you?"

The old man's rheumy eyes dropped to Bannion's face. They were sharp and scathing in their long regard. "What's the matter, Doyle . . . can't they stand having their thick Texas hides pricked a little? Seems to me that's exactly what those four have been needing for a long time."

"All the same, why not just let bygones be bygones?" Bannion said.

The doctor went to the door, threw a little nod to Judith, then turned and owlishly winked at Bannion. "They won't shoot me, Sheriff. They're too curious about what went on between their pappy and me. Besides, what hell-roaring young Texan would be proud of shooting an old bent-over doctor?"

Bannion opened his mouth to say something, but the doctor left the room. Bannion looked glumly over at Judith and wagged his head. She looked faintly amused.

Bannion slapped his knees and leaned forward as though to arise. "Well, Miss Judy, you lived through something you can tell your grand-children."

She let that pass, saying instead: "Sheriff, please don't go just yet. I want to talk to you."

Bannion leaned back in the sofa, looking and waiting. She was very lovely there with her softly shining blonde hair that fell down across both shoulders and made a background for the even-ness, the flushed rosiness of her face.

"Why did those men do that for me, Sheriff?"

Bannion looked astonished. He attempted an answer: "Why? Well . . . why not? I mean, you were lost and all, and they . . ."

"Sheriff, you know perfectly well how my father feels toward them. What he intends to do to them. You know I left no doubts with them about how I felt about them, either, for killing our ranch foreman."

"Well sure," said Bannion, trying to organize his thoughts. "But, Miss Judy, that's different. That's a personal thing. A private fight. They feel plumb justified in that. But with you, it was different . . . you were lost out in the storm and maybe dying, and they just naturally went to help."

"I've been thinking, Sheriff. If they'd left me to die out there . . . they could have hurt my father the worst possible way."

"Miss Judy, those men have no quarrel with your paw. It was McAfee they wanted . . . and they got him. If that dog-gone Santa Ana hadn't come along, they'd be maybe sixty miles from Perdition Wells by now. They never wanted to hurt your paw. They don't want to hurt him now, Miss Judy."

"Sheriff, could you get them out of town right away?"

Bannion eased back in the sofa, stretching out his legs. He shook his head. "They're near blind.

Anyway, they shouldn't be out in the bright sun for at least a few days."

"My father will be looking for me, Sheriff. Sooner or later he'll come here, and he'll be told the King brothers are still in town. You know what that means, don't you?"

"Yes, I know," retorted Bannion. "And I've been thinking about it. But the Kings can't be moved without endangering them." Bannion looked up. "I thought maybe you could influence your paw, Miss Judy. After all, they *did* save your life."

"I've also thought of that, and I'll try. But, Sheriff, what if I fail?"

Bannion pushed himself up out of the sofa, took up his hat, and turned it gravely in his fingers. "I'm betting you won't fail," he said, and went over to the door. There he changed the subject, saying: "By the way, you haven't told me how you happened to be out where we found you."

Judith shrugged as though that wasn't important now. "The storm caught me just beyond town. I tried to turn back, but when the wind hit my horse, he wouldn't turn his face into it. I tried to fight him around. He bucked me off. That fall knocked the wind out of me. I tried to get up, when I was all right again, but by then the Santa Ana was raging and I couldn't even crawl. I tried until I just couldn't move another inch, then I guess I fainted. The next thing I recall is seeing you bending over me at your office."

Bannion nodded. "That's why your eyes didn't get it like ours did, I expect. You were face down when we found you. Well, Miss Judy, I've got more calls to make, but I'll be back."

"Sheriff? Please get them out of town, or at least hide them where my father's men can't find them."

Bannion opened the door and gently shook his head. "I'd hide them in a minute, Miss Judy, but they aren't the hiding kind and I'm only one man."

"Then arrest them. Take their guns away and put guards outside their room."

Bannion stood stockstill for a moment, turning this suggestion over in his mind. He said, finally and quietly: "Darned if you haven't hit the nail smack dab on the head. That's the solution I've been searching for."

He left the girl's room feeling much better, went downstairs to the lobby, approached several lounging range men there, called them together, and formally deputized all of them. There were five of these men, and none of them offered any objection to being deputized. They were cowboys between jobs and a deputy's pay of $1 a day and ammunition, even if it was only for a day or two, was welcome to them.

Bannion told them only that they were to sit outside an upstairs room and admit no one unless Bannion himself was there to sanction admittance. He did not tell these men that the prisoners were the same men John Rockland of the powerful Texas Star outfit was seeking for the shooting of Dale McAfee.

Upstairs again, Bannion positioned his new deputies. With grins these five hard-bitten riders got chairs, cocked them back against the wall outside the room of the King brothers, and began their lazy vigil.

Bannion went inside. The doctor had been there and gone. Austin was busy at a wash basin and the air smelled strongly of medication. The youngest King shot Bannion a slow, slightly restrained smile.

"Darned if I ever thought I'd see the day I was a nurse," he said.

Bannion did not smile back. He looked at the three men in this room with wet cloths over their eyes. He also looked over where their shell belts and holstered weapons were carelessly hanging over the back of a chair. He counted those gun belts, saw that all four were there, and went forward, removed each weapon, hung them all by their trigger guards from the fingers of his left hand. He turned toward Austin, whose back was to him, with his own gun in his right hand.

Austin turned around with a cloth in his hands —and froze.

"Sheriff," he said, "what the hell do you think you're doing? Put down those guns."

The three other men shifted in their beds, sweeping away their bandages and stonily staring at Bannion. Al's eyes were swollen entirely closed, but, by using both hands, he pried them open the slightest bit. This caused pain and Al's hard cursing was the only sound in the room. Hank and Ray were in better shape.

Ray said: "Sheriff, you better do like Austin says. Put those guns down."

Bannion went sideways toward the door. When Austin would have moved to intercept him, Bannion swung his pistol barrel and Austin stopped in his tracks.

"Boys, you're under arrest. There are five men outside in the hallway with orders to let no one out of here . . . and no one in here."

"Arrest!" exploded Hank. "Arrest for what?"

Bannion said easily: "I'm not sure just yet, but I'll think of something."

The four of them stared. Austin looked at Ray as though seeking a signal of some kind. Ray sat there gazing ahead at Bannion without speaking. He finally made a gentle little head wag at Austin and the youngest of them relaxed.

In his quiet way, Ray said: "All right, Bannion, you've got a reason for doing this. What is it?"

"To keep you alive."

"From Rockland?"

"Yes."

Al growled from his cot. "Just leave those guns

here and you won't have to worry about us . . . or Rockland."

"That's why I'm taking them with me. Because I *am* worrying about that, Al. No more killings."

Ray sighed. "Bannion, you're holding the wrong men. We're about helpless right now. The man you should stop and disarm is Rockland . . . not us."

"Rockland's not in town and you boys are."

"Well, if he isn't in town," Hank began, but got no further.

Bannion cut across his words. "He's found Judy's horse by now and my guess is that he's searching the range for her. When he doesn't find her, he'll come to town. That's all the time I have to get organized for him."

"You could go out and see him before he gets here," grumbled Al.

"No, I can't take the chance of him riding in here while I'm gone."

Ray leaned back on his bed. He put both arms under his head, pushed his legs out to their full distance, and relaxed. Al and Hank took their cue from him, also relaxing. Young Austin looked bitterly at the sheriff for some time, but then he, too, turned his back and resumed working at the wash basin.

Ray said: "Tell me something, Bannion. How's Miss Judy?"

"A lot better than you fellers. At least she looks a lot better."

"She sure does," murmured Ray, and turned to show Bannion a little quirked-up smile. "One more question. Is she still mad at us?"

Bannion let his muscles turn loose but he did not lower his gun. "About tomorrow," he said to Ray King, "you can go ask her that yourself. She didn't tell me whether she's still sore or not." Bannion kept staring at Ray. He had a dawning notion knocking around inside his head. He was remembering how Ray and Judith had stood staring at each other in the hallway. How he had stubbornly refused to let Al assist in carrying her back to town during the storm. Bannion was a bachelor with little knowledge of the intricacies of a man-woman relationship, but in his lifetime he had seen many men with that same soft and distant expression on their faces that was now settled over the handsome and rugged countenance of the eldest of the King boys.

"Well," Austin said suddenly, sharply, "what are you staring at, Sheriff? You got our guns . . . what more do you want?"

Bannion looked at Austin only briefly. He returned his gaze to Ray. "Your word you won't try to leave this room."

Hank hooted at this. "You got no charge against us, and you expect us to lie here like a gang of sheep waiting for Rockland to come boiling in here with his gun crew all primed for bear. Sheriff, you're being kind of childish."

"How about it, Ray?" asked Bannion. "Your word?"

All eyes went to the eldest brother and remained there, waiting. Ray made no immediate answer. He first lowered his arms, sat up on the edge of his cot, and looked upon Bannion without any expression showing at all.

"We'll promise you this," he said finally. "If you keep Rockland and his men out of here, we won't go looking for them. But, Sheriff, if they bust in here past those guards of yours, we'll promise you only one thing . . . the damnedest fight you ever saw here in Perdition Wells. Is that fair enough?"

Bannion thought it was and said so.

"Then," said Ray, "leave us our guns. Because if you don't . . . and Rockland gets in here somehow . . . you'll be even guiltier of our murders than he will be."

"I absolutely have the word of each of you?" Bannion persisted in asking.

"That we won't try to leave this room? Yes," replied Ray.

Bannion put their guns down upon a table and left.

Chapter Twelve

John Rockland and his men rode into Perdition Wells after full nightfall. A little wind still riffled tin roofs and stirred dust in the roadway but the Santa Ana's real force was entirely gone now. The orange lamplight puddled beyond stores and saloons, making those riding men alternately bright and dark as they went along to Bannion's office and dismounted.

Rockland alone entered the jailhouse. His riders remained outside with the horses, looking thirstily over where saloon lights shone and where sounds of revelry were strong again.

Bannion was not surprised when John Rockland came in. He had expected him even earlier, before sundown or shortly thereafter. He thought privately that Rockland looked bad. There were gray knots of slack flesh under his eyes and the arrogance, the yeasty pride, was wiped out of the big cowman's dull stare.

"Judy's lost," said Rockland, giving Bannion no chance to speak first. "Her horse came to the ranch without her. I organized search parties, but we haven't found any trace of her."

"She's over at the hotel," Bannion informed him, and saw how Rockland's eyes kept widening, staring down at him. "She got bucked off right after she struck out for home, Mister Rockland, and her horse ran on. We found . . ."

Rockland struck the floor hard with both his booted feet. He whirled, flung back Bannion's heavy door, and plunged out into the night. He went past his astonished cowboys without seeing them and in a twinkling disappeared into the hotel shouldering aside anyone in his way.

Bannion went out to the riders. "I told him Miss Judy's safe at the hotel. It hit him like a ton of bricks."

One of those Texas Star men fixed Bannion with a baleful look. "I tried to tell him she'd have more sense than try to ride home from here . . . but he wouldn't listen. He liked to rode our tail bones raw searchin' every blessed inch of the range. Sheriff, we been in the saddle since before that danged storm blew itself out, and, as far as I can figure, we'll be there for another couple hours."

Bannion nodded. An idea occurred to him. "Why don't you go on home?" he said. "He'll likely want someone to go on back and tell Judy's mother, anyway." Bannion stood, watching those tired faces, waiting.

One man looked at his companion. He said: "Why not? Mister Rockland'll be up there with his girl for a long while. He might even forget we're waitin' out here. What d'you say? Let's go."

An older rider, craggy, disgruntled, and slit-eyed, a man named Carl Arnold who Bannion had known casually for the five years he'd worked for Texas Star, said growlingly: "Naw. If Rockland comes out an' we was gone, he'd raise hell an' prop it up. You fellers know how he's been these last couple o' days. Naw. We'd better just stand around and wait."

Bannion's hopes for getting Texas Star out of town dwindled. He stood there, looking at those tired cowboys, scarcely conscious that the grizzled rider was speaking again. Then, when the man's grumbling words sank in, Bannion drew upright off the hitch rack, staring.

"An' besides," Carl Arnold was continuing on, "he's supposed to meet them three fellers he telegraphed for to come here in town and he'll want to see to that."

"What three men?" Bannion asked.

The Texas Star riders looked at him. Their tired faces blanked over one at a time, turning expressionless, turning impassive. They made no answer, and after a while they looked accusingly at Carl Arnold as though his weariness had allowed him to say something careless, something he never should have said.

"What three men, I asked you?"

Arnold mumbled something indistinguishable and looked uncomfortable. He eventually said: "Replacements for them fellers who rode off yesterday when the King boys called us in the roadway."

"Like hell," Bannion snorted. "You could have hired twenty replacement riders right here in town, Carl. You didn't have to telegraph for more hands."

"Maybe Mister Rockland didn't think of that," Arnold said lamely.

Bannion closed his lips. He looked at those tired but dogged faces. He said to Carl Arnold: "Are you replacing McAfee as Texas Star's foreman?"

Arnold nodded.

"Then let me give you some advice, Carl. The first gunfighter who rides in here looking for the King brothers is going to run head-on into a brick wall, and if any Texas Star men are with him, they're going to get into the same trouble up to their ears."

"Who said anything about gunfighters," growled Arnold. "I only said Mister Rockland . . ."

"Oh for the love of Mike, quit making it worse," Bannion snapped, and started around the hitch rack. He saw Arnold nod to one of his men and saw that man come forward to intercept him. Bannion turned, going into a slight forward crouch. The cowboy stopped still. There was irresolution on his face and because of this feeling he instantly lost the initiative.

"Don't," Bannion warned. "Don't try it." They hung there a moment, Bannion facing the lot of them. Then he turned and went swiftly on across the road toward the hotel. He stepped swiftly over to the stairwell and climbed the steps swiftly. At Judy's door Bannion paused a second, heard no voices, and knocked. Judy's voice called for him to enter and Bannion did so.

The girl was sitting up in bed looking curious. When she saw her visitor was Bannion, some of this interest atrophied.

"Where's your paw, Miss Judy?"

"He left a few minutes ago, Sheriff. He went to talk to the Kings."

Bannion's tightness began to atrophy. He sighed and leaned upon the wall saying: "You talked to him?"

"Yes. He wanted to hear the story from the Kings, about how they brought me back to town." Judy smiled. "I think your troubles are over, Sheriff Bannion."

"I sure hope so," Bannion responded. "I sure hope so. Well, I'll go see my prisoners."

Judy's level dark gaze twinkled. "Did you arrest them . . . really, Sheriff?"

"Well, sort of. I made them promise not to leave their room."

Judy's twinkle softened. She was quiet for a moment, putting a sentence together, then finally said: "Maybe Ray could come see me. I mean, as you said, I should thank him, shouldn't I?"

"Oh," Bannion answered at once, "of course you

should, Miss Judy. That'd only be good manners."

"Uh . . . you could tell him, Sheriff?"

Without showing anything on his face, Bannion made a little gallant bow. "It'd be my pleasure," he answered, and left the room. Outside the door, Bannion stood still for a minute, letting an understanding small smile form around his lips. Then he went forward where his five deputized range men loafed before the door of the room of the King brothers.

As Bannion came up, the roughest-looking of those deputies cocked an eye at him. "Say, Sheriff," he said in a lazy drawl, "why didn't you tell us them fellers inside were the same ones who shot McAfee?"

"What's the difference? You agreed to do a job, didn't you?"

"Yeah, we agreed. And we're doin' it. Only John Rockland come a-stormin' up here a little bit ago, an' when we refused to let him in, he exploded."

"Exploded?"

"Yeah. He said regardless of what the Kings done for his daughter they were cowards to hire men to guard them."

"You told him I put you here, didn't you?"

The cowboy shrugged. "He never give us that chance. He went stormin' along the hallway like we'd personally insulted him."

"I just came up," Bannion said, "and I didn't meet him."

"He went along to the rear staircase and down the back way, Sheriff."

Bannion whirled, went trotting to the yonder stairs, and descended them two at a time. He passed hurriedly across the lobby and hit the sidewalk just in time to hear Rockland and his Texas Star riders go rushing northward out of town.

Bannion was standing there, his expression congealing with anger, when the doctor came strolling along on his way upstairs.

He said: "Doyle, this world's full of men who operate on snap judgments. I just saw John Rockland ride past at a lope and his face was all red with what looked to me like indignation."

"He," Bannion pronounced shortly, "is a big damned fool."

"Oh," the doctor agreed, "you'd never get an argument from me on that score. But I've often wondered how long it would be before John Rockland got his humbling."

"Did you now," Bannion said, turning his wrathful look upon the medical man. "Well, let me tell you something . . . he won't get it in my town, if I can prevent it. And that, Doctor, is a fact!"

The medical man shot his rheumy eyes up the roadway. He pursed his lips, and after a time he said: "Doyle, you're a good man. But the good men in this world rarely win . . . unless they happen to be the strong men, also." He lowered his gaze. "And there's something odd about

138

strength . . . whether it derives from wealth or plain power, it corrupts the good men. Now John Rockland's had wealth and power a long time, Doyle. He's not a bad man, really, but power has corrupted him. If I were in your boots, I'd just stand aside a little and let him get his humbling. It just might make a human being out of him again. Hell, I've a notion to get together a posse and go after Rockland myself."

"Go take care of your confounded patients," Bannion growled, and he stood, waiting until the doctor had gone into the hotel before making some very grisly statements under his breath. He then struck out for the telegraph office.

The telegrapher was a stolid, middle-aged man imbued with great dignity, great esteem for himself as Perdition Wells' keeper of the talking wire. His ethics were unimpeachable, his sense of duty was unassailable, and his mind was as hidebound and narrow and tight as the minds of transplanted New Englanders usually are. He viewed Sheriff Bannion askance as the lawman burst into his office, continued at his work the prescribed amount of time so that Bannion would be properly impressed, then he eased back in his chair and peered upward from beneath a green eye-shade.

Bannion said bluntly: "I want to see every telegram John Rockland has sent from here in the past week."

The telegrapher sat on, saying nothing and firming up his look of outrage. "Messages are confidential information, Sheriff. No one has the right to . . ."

"Mister, you dig those telegrams out right damned now or I'll come around this counter and get them myself."

The telegrapher's neck turned turkey red. He clenched a pale fist and glared. "Without a court order you wouldn't dare," he said, and started to get up. A sharp little snippet of sound froze him in mid-motion. He was looking head-on into the solitary black, eyeless socket of Bannion's cocked six-gun.

"I'll count to three," Bannion warned, and pushed his gun over the counter. "One . . . two . . ."

Angrily the telegrapher began to sort through the pale yellow slips of paper. He put aside three messages as he came to them. "Here," he said, choking with indignation. "My home office will hear about this, Sheriff. By God, no man can . . ."

"Shut up," Bannion snarled. Then he holstered his weapon and placed the copies of the telegrams side-by-side. "One to someone named Brady Elam at the Porter House over in Round Rock. One to a man named Butch Hobart at the same address, and a third one to a man named Hodge Fuller at Flat Rock." Bannion looked up. "Same messages in each case. 'Come at once. Two thousand dollars your pay.' They're all signed by Rockland." He looked steadily at the telegrapher. For several minutes neither man said a word.

Then Bannion repeated those names: "Elam, Hobart, Fuller." He pushed the telegram copies away. "Thanks," he said with hard irony. "Now you go ahead and wire your head office, if you like. Tell them you're a party to planned murder, too. Those three men are professional gunfighters John Rockland is bringing here to kill four men."

Bannion left the office.

Behind him the telegrapher sat staring. Then he rose up, leaned upon the counter, and studied each of the three wires he had sent. After that he sank back down in his chair and thought over what had happened. He decided not to forward any complaint against Sheriff Bannion after all.

Bannion went to his office, heated water on his iron stove to shave himself. After he was finished, he sat for a long time smoking at his desk. He kept thinking over what the doctor had said about John Rockland needing a humbling. Bannion had considered getting together a posse and riding to Texas Star to arrest Rockland. He considered this very seriously.

What deterred him was the realization that in his absence Rockland's hired killers would arrive in Perdition Wells. They'd had ample time to get here, even allowing for the delay no doubt caused by the Santa Ana.

Bannion also considered going to see Rockland alone, of telling Rockland exactly what he thought of a man who would deliberately prosecute his vendetta even after the men he was angry at had saved his daughter's life.

But again, that idea involved leaving town since Rockland and his men had headed back to the Texas Star. So Bannion sat there, thinking fierce thoughts that were slowly coming to a steady boil, while around him in the night Perdition Wells, considering the recent windstorm its only threat, celebrated its passing with excessive exuberance at the saloons and dance halls.

Bannion looked at his watch, made himself a cup of coffee, and decided he would, after a while, go over and join his deputies outside the hotel room of the King brothers.

He had one thing in his favor. He did not really believe that Rockland would now go through with his plan to have the Kings gunned down. Besides, none of those telegrams had named the men Rockland meant for the gunfighters to seek out. The hired killers, therefore, had to go see Rockland before going after the King boys, and, if Bannion's hunch was right, he thought Rockland would pay them for their time and send them on their way again.

What annoyed him most was the way Rockland had ridden out of town without even thanking him for his part in saving Judy. If he'd done that, if he'd made any attempt at all to see Bannion before departing, the sheriff could have, he thought, clinched what Judy had told her father concerning the great debt of gratitude Rockland owed the four men from west Texas.

"He's too big," Bannion said aloud in the emptiness of his office. "He's just too damned big and uppity, like Doc says. He's the center of the universe and all the rest of humanity is the herd of little stars that revolve around him. For a plugged copper I'd go release those Kings and tell them what he's gone and done. I think John Rockland would get taught one helluva lesson real fast." Bannion finished his coffee, hit the floor hard with his booted feet as he rose up, and said savagely: "Damn!"

He dragged on his hat and went slamming out into the cool, early night, scuffing at the roadway dust on his way to the hotel.

Chapter Thirteen

The five deputies outside the King door were hungry, bored, and restless. Bannion could and did alleviate the first of these problems by sending the cowboys two at a time to eat. He and the rough-looking, oldest of these men were the last pair to go.

They went to the Shafter Café, had their supper, and sat talking over coffee and a smoke.

"Seems to me," said the deputy, as he leaned upon the table replete and pensive, "you'd ought to just let them fellers be on their way, Sheriff."

"Day after tomorrow," Bannion said sarcastically. "One way or another they'll probably be traveling day after tomorrow."

"Day after tomorrow?"

"Haven't you seen them?"

"No. They don't come out. When they wanted food, they hollered an' we brought it."

"Well, their eyes are bad off from rescuing Rockland's daughter during the Santa Ana. Doc's orders. They have to keep out of bright light for a few days."

This appeared to amuse the cowboy. He said: "That's pretty sound advice at that, for when John Rockland comes for them, they're goin' to need lots of darkness to maneuver around in."

"Let's go back," Bannion snapped, leading the way out of the café. Outside, he squinted, then he said: "You're making a pretty common mistake, pardner. You're judging men before you know anything about them."

"Yeah? You mean them King boys?"

"I do. And the reason I'm keeping them in their room is because Rockland, not them, might need a lot of darkness, if he goes after them."

They walked along slowly and were almost to the hotel before the cowboy said: "Hell, Sheriff . . . are they really that rough?"

"Stick around," Bannion informed the man. "I've got a bad feeling you're going to find out."

Upstairs, the deputies spelled one another so they could rest. They accomplished this by the simple expedient of going down to the lobby, selecting the most comfortable chair, stretching themselves out there, tilting up their hats, and going to sleep. The clerk was less than elated over this arrangement of Bannion's, particularly since two of these rough men proved to be prodigious snorers, but he was a prudent man and said nothing.

In this fashion the night passed.

Bannion left the hotel and went to his office about dawn. He fell onto a pallet in one of his little cells and slept like a baby until, near noon, the doctor appeared to awaken him, brew up and help himself to some of Bannion's coffee, and preëmpt Bannion's desk chair.

While the sheriff washed, the medical man mused aloud, comfortable where he sat and pensive. "You know, Doyle, I put in a long two hours with your prisoners over at the hotel."

"Did you, now."

"Yep. I talked until my tongue ran dry. Did you know those boys hardly even knew their pappy?"

"I guessed that, yes."

"They pumped me dry about him."

"And you told them everything?"

"Well . . . almost everything."

Bannion and the doctor exchanged a look, then Bannion resumed washing.

"I also told them there's another old gaffer from King's Confederate Raiders hereabouts."

This time Bannion put aside the towel and looked hard at the older man. "Name him," he ordered.

"Rufus Paige."

"Doc, how long've you known about Rufus?"

"Four, five months. Why?"

Bannion said curtly: "Nothing. Forget I asked."

"Be glad to," chirped the doctor, not the least curious. "I also told those boys something their paw said to me once. 'Henry,' he says to me, 'wars don't end with the last shot or the last bugle call. They live on, dying out very gradually, and in their wake all manner of hateful things happen.

Our war has been especially bad that way . . . Rebs still hate Yanks. Our children grow up with that. If I had my way every veteran would have to take an oath never to talk of the war. He'd have to swear on the Good Book never to cuss a Yank where children could hear him.' "

Bannion was standing perfectly motionless. He said softly: "You told his sons that?"

"I did."

"And what was their reaction?"

"They just sat there looking at me, Doyle. Never said a word . . . just sat there looking at me."

Bannion put his hat back on. He walked slowly over in front of the doctor. He said solemnly: "That's the only wise thing that's come out of this whole blessed affair, Doc. I'm obliged to you. I think you've made my job easier."

The medical man nodded. "Thought it might do that," he said, and got up. "I need a drink. I've talked more this morning than I've talked in five years and it makes me dry as a bone."

Bannion thought of something, and said: "Doc, would you do me a favor?"

"It's possible," replied the old man, beginning to look cautious. "It's possible, Doyle. What is it?"

"Get in your buggy, ride out to Texas Star, and tell John Rockland I want him to come here and stop those gunfighters he hired. Tell him . . ."

"Gunfighters?"

Bannion nodded and parted his lips to resume

speaking. The doctor's face turned dark and thunderous. He cut across the sheriff's voice with a reedy, wrathful tone of his own.

"Gunfighters? Did that hawk-nosed devil actually hire gunfighters? Why damn his lights, Doyle Bannion, damn his lights! You mean to stand there and tell me that after those four boys saved Judith's life, he still has the gall to hire them killed? Now I'll not stand for that. Come hell or high water, I'll not stand for that."

"Listen, Doc . . ."

"Listen nothing. That's all I've been doing . . . listening. First to you, then to Judith, then to the King boys. Now I've listened all I'm going to. Doyle, I have friends hereabouts. Good friends, too. I saved a few lives here and there in my time. Doyle Bannion, you bet I'll go out to Texas Star, damned if I won't, and I'll take twenty armed men with me, too, and we'll see about this hiring gunfighters business."

Then the doctor stormed out of Bannion's office, shaking his head fiercely, as Bannion tried to reason with him. The medico didn't stop, just kept stomping along the boardwalk, still raging aloud in his squeaky old voice.

Bannion stood in front of the jailhouse watching. He stepped back as far as a wall bench and sank down there. He was disgusted with himself. He'd known the doctor was an old firebrand. He'd seen him roiled up before, but never like this, never actually making threats and plans to carry them out. This, he told himself, is just what I needed—a band of hotheads storming the Texas Star and reading the riot act to John Rockland. He would have to stop the doctor before he got under way, even if that meant locking him in a cell. Bannion got up, and started forward.

"Hey, Sheriff!"

Bannion halted and turned. It was Sam Ryan from the livery barn. Sam was walking hurriedly —a very unusual thing for him—and his face was very solemn. He came up to the sheriff and halted, breathing hard and speaking in a low tone.

"Sheriff, three fellers just put up their horses at the barn. They come into town from different directions, but that didn't fool me none. You could tell they knew one another . . . only they tried to act like they didn't. Sheriff, they're gunfighters if ever I seen any, and believe you me in my sixty-six years I've seen plenty of 'em. More'n enough to know 'em when I see 'em, and that's a fact."

Bannion forgot all about the doctor. "Three of 'em, eh?" he said, throwing a look along the roadway. "Where are they now?"

"When I left the barn, they was standin' outside talkin' to Carl Arnold."

Bannion was surprised. "Carl Arnold? You mean that rider from Texas Star?"

"The same. Him an' old Rufus Paige just come into town with the supply wagon from Rockland's."

Bannion left Ryan standing there. He went along as far as the general store, past it, and then around to the rear alleyway where he espied the Texas Star wagon backed up to a doorway. The process of loading was already in progress.

Bannion squeezed over the tailgate, entered the store, and walked all the way out front before he saw old Rufus standing with the proprietor, his face puckered up as he struggled to read the long list in his hands. Rufus was holding this paper as though by sheer strength alone he would compel it to disgorge its written words.

Bannion pushed the storekeeper aside, whirled Rufus around, and said sharply: "Where is Arnold?"

Rufus turned angrily and jerked his arm out of Bannion's grip. "How do I know where he is?" he demanded. "I ain't his wet nurse. He met three fellers outside the livery barn and told me to come over here and load up the wagon. He's gone to wet his cussed whistle for all I know. An' you keep your hands off . . ."

"Three gunfighters, Rufus . . . not three fellows. Three gunhands John Rockland sent for to kill the King boys."

Rufus's anger disappeared in an instant. He blinked at Bannion, saying slowly: "Sheriff, do you know what you're sayin'?"

But Bannion was already moving toward the front roadway and did not reply.

Rufus looked after him a moment, then jack-knifed into action. Pushing the list of supplies into the slack-jawed storekeeper's hand, he bellowed—"Wait for me!"—and went hobbling as rapidly as his crippled legs would permit, in pursuit of Sheriff Bannion. At the doorway, remembering his obligation to Texas Star, he twisted and called back: "Load the wagon with them things! I can't stay to help you, but, even if I could, it wouldn't much matter 'cause I can't hardly read anyhow."

Bannion went first to the livery barn. He was already a good two hundred yards ahead of Rufus Paige, when he was told the three strangers were no longer around. Next he struck out for the nearest saloon to the livery, and he lost old Rufus entirely.

The gunfighters were nowhere to be found in this bar. Bannion spent thirty minutes going from saloon to saloon. When he found himself near the hotel, he went upstairs there to check with his guards. They had seen no strangers, nor anyone else for that matter, they told Bannion.

Bannion went back down to the roadway and stood there, thinking, looking north and south. He was stumped. It was as though the earth had opened up and swallowed Rockland's new range boss, along with his three hired killers.

"Hey, Sheriff . . . !"

It was Rufus, puffing from exertion and looking indignant. Bannion let him catch up. "Where are they?" the Texas Star's cook asked. "Consarn it . . . there's no need to rush around like a chicken with its head shot off, is there? We'll find 'em."

Bannion was angry and he showed it now. "We'll do nothing. *You* go on back to your wagon and don't get involved in this. You hear me, Rufus?"

"I'd have to be deaf not to," growled the old man. "Two heads are better'n one, Bannion. You heard that ol' sayin', ain't you?"

Bannion purpled. He glared at Rufus, then he said in a whipsaw tone: "Get! Go on back to your wagon! Damn you, Rufus, if it hadn't been for you, I wouldn't have this mess on my hands. Two heads better'n one. . . . Dog-gone you for an old meddler, anyway. Now scat, or I'll use my boot toe to start you out."

Rufus blinked before he moved back a few cautious feet where he continued to stare. "Never seen you so mad before," he muttered. "All right, Sheriff, I'm goin'. No need to be nasty . . . I'm goin'."

From fifty feet along the plank walk Rufus turned, put his indignant eyes upon Bannion, and hesitated there, obviously considering the sheriff's words and a response to them. In the end though, he kept them to himself, wheeled around, and went stiffly back toward the general store.

Chapter Fourteen

Something was wrong here and Bannion knew it. He stood on the plank walk with the afternoon bustle going on around him, seeing the people of his town, hearing them at their chores. He felt that the recent windstorm was all that occupied their conversation, while a big black cloud of real trouble was steadily building up over their heads of which they were totally ignorant.

He went back to the livery barn, had Sam Ryan show him the horses and outfits of the three newcomers. All three horses wore the same brand. These men were not, as Sam had opined, strangers to one another at all.

Under the livery man's worried eye Bannion rummaged through the bedrolls and saddlebags of each man. He found nothing in the first two, but in the third one he found a copy of John Rockland's telegram. Ryan read this over Bannion's shoulder and gasped.

"Be damned," he said. "Mister Rockland sent for 'em."

Bannion pocketed the telegram and crossed the road to the first saloon he'd entered in his earlier search. There he unexpectedly came upon Carl Arnold idly drinking cool beer at the bar.

Arnold seemed deep in thought and somewhat troubled. Bannion stepped up beside him, ignored the barman, and said: "Carl, I want to know where those gunmen are."

Arnold straightened up, looking astonished. For a moment he simply stared, then he said in a hollow tone: "What gunmen, Sheriff?"

Bannion checked an impulse to say something fierce. "Don't play games with me, Carl." He shook out the telegram, watched Arnold read it, then he put it back into his pocket. "*Those* gunmen, and unless you tell me within two minutes I'm going to arrest you."

Arnold pushed his emptied beer glass away. He twisted from the waist so that he was facing Bannion. He had made a decision and Bannion could see in the resolution upon his face that good or bad he was going to stand by it.

"Don't ask me nothing, Sheriff. If you want answers, go see Mister Rockland. He's probably at the ranch."

"What d'you mean probably. Don't you know where he is?"

"No," said Arnold. "I haven't seen him since last night. After we got back to the ranch last night he told me to come to town with Rufus an' the supply wagon this morning. I ain't seen him today."

Bannion was at once struck with an idea. He said: "Carl, what did Mister Rockland tell you fellers after he went storming out of town last night?"

Arnold shook his head. "Nothing. He rode all the way back without saying a word. He was mad . . . we could see that . . . but he'd been pushing himself and us too dog-gone hard for over twenty-four hours, so didn't none of us pay much attention. He went into the house the second he got home, and we hit the bunkhouse."

Bannion's idea was becoming a slow conviction.

"Carl, you listen to me. Last night Judy tried to talk her paw into forgetting his private feud with the King boys over McAfee's killing. She told me he actually went to see the Kings with maybe an idea of apologizing to them, or at least thanking them. But whatever he had in mind, it wasn't more fighting."

"He didn't say anything like that to us, Sheriff."

"Just shut up and listen. I had guards outside the room where the Kings are. They roiled Rockland, I guess . . . anyway, he went fuming out to you boys and led you out of town in a big rush."

Arnold considered. He shrugged, beginning to frown. "I don't know anything about any of this, Sheriff. All I know is that I take my orders from Mister Rockland, and a couple of days ago he told me . . ." Arnold closed his mouth and deepened his dogged scowl.

Bannion nodded. "I'll finish that for you," he

said. "Rockland told you he'd sent for three gunfighters. He told you why he'd sent for them . . . to avenge McAfee. Today, when you rode into town with Rufus, you saw three strangers over at the livery barn and you figured, if these were the gunmen, you'd save them riding out to get their orders straight from John Rockland, so you went over, told them you were Rockland's foreman, and told them what Rockland wanted. Carl, you gave them he names of the Kings."

Arnold took up his empty beer glass and peered into it. He set it down and looked around for the barman. When the apron-covered barkeep came forth, Arnold indicated he wanted a refill.

At his side Bannion watched all this, waiting. Finally Arnold turned, looking harassed.

"Try and prove any of that," he growled at Bannion. "I take orders from the man who pays me, and what he says is good enough for me."

"You're a fool!" exclaimed Bannion. "Since last night things have changed. If you had a brain inside your skull, you'd know that's a fact. Rockland doesn't want the King boys killed now . . . they saved the life of his only child."

"All I know," Arnold said stubbornly, "is what he told me a couple of days ago . . . after Dale McAfee's killing."

"Yeah," Bannion said disgustedly, "so now you've put those gunhawks to work, and you've

156

put John Rockland in one helluva spot. All right, Carl, you've done what you thought you had to do. Now I'm going to undo that and save your stupid neck for you. Where are those gunfighters?"

"I don't know."

"You're a liar!"

Arnold came around in a flash, his eyes flaming.

Bannion was ready. He had stepped away from the bar as he'd hurled those fighting words. He was standing, wide-legged and bent inward slightly from the shoulders now, waiting.

"Go ahead," he said to Arnold. "Go on, Carl, make your play."

But Carl Arnold, not an intelligent man, was mixed up in his mind. He was not basically a bad, or even a mean, man. He was fearful Bannion's words might be true and he was beginning to worry over what he'd done. He hung there, undecided, and indecision in a gunfight was the worst possible attitude. Very gradually the rigidity left Arnold's spine, his arm straightened, and he drew up erect. His expression was more troubled now than angry.

He said: "I'm going to get me a livery horse and go back to the ranch."

"You do that," agreed Bannion, also coming up out of his crouch. "And you'd better make a fast trip of it, too, because if anything happens while you're gone, it won't just be you that's in hot water up to his neck, it'll also be John Rockland."

"I'll find out," Arnold said, and started away.

Bannion halted him briefly with his question: "Where are those gunfighters? This is the last time I'm going to ask you that, Carl."

But Arnold, like most people who operated almost entirely by instinct, had closed his mind around this one thing like iron. He could have been dragged behind wild horses, but he never would have volunteered this information. He only glared balefully at Bannion, then pushed on out of the saloon, leaving Bannion standing there, wondering whether to go after him, or let him rush back to Texas Star.

In the end Bannion thought Arnold's return to Texas Star was more important than any additional delay, so he turned, leaned upon the bar, and his warm gaze fell upon Arnold's untouched glass of beer. He lifted it, drained it dry, and slammed the glass down.

The barman shuffled up, put forth a tentative smile, and said: "Sheriff, when them fellers was in here with Carl, I couldn't help but hear a little of what they was talkin' about."

"Yeah," Bannion muttered dryly. "One thing about barmen . . . they got awful good ears. I don't suppose you heard them say where they were going, though."

"I heard that, yes. Carl told them the King brothers had a room at the hotel."

Bannion was puzzled. His deputies had said no one had approached them. Suddenly it struck Bannion and he started in his tracks. The back stairway. He had not placed any guard there, believing it would be unnecessary, but now he recalled how a rickety fire escape of checked wood ran along the hotel's rear. Access to this fire escape, which went along beneath the windows of each upstairs room, was by that back stairway.

Bannion rushed out of the saloon, turned south, and went ahead to a little passageway between two buildings. He hastened along this toward the rear alleyway leading down behind the hotel.

Back at the saloon, the barman stood mournfully considering that emptied beer glass. Both Arnold and Bannion had drunk from it, yet neither of them had paid. *If a thing like this becomes a habit, a feller could go out of business,* he thought to himself, picking up the glass. He was still standing there, viewing the glass when the gunshots came, exploding into the afternoon quiet like cannon.

Bannion was nearly through the dogtrot and into the yonder alleyway when he heard the shots. He knew at once that while he'd been trying to winnow information from Carl Arnold time had run out on him. Instead of springing erect as everyone else did who heard those blasting explosions, Bannion ran harder, hurtled out into the alleyway, turned to his right, and went along

159

toward the rear of the hotel. It had initially been his hope to catch the gunmen halfway up the hotel's back wall, exposed upon that old outside staircase. Now though, as a veritable fusillade of gunshots erupted, he knew the hired killers had gotten inside the hotel.

When he came down through the afternoon shadows behind the hotel and glanced up, the fire escape was empty. He wasted no second glance but rushed the rear entrance to that building, went charging into the pantry, encountered a wide-eyed waitress there, and shot past her on through the dining room and into the adjacent lobby.

Here, people were milling, speaking shrilly, and looking at one another, dumbfounded. From overhead, there came several rattling shots that sounded thunderously loud within the building and made the windows rattle noisily in their casings. The hotel clerk shot a beseeching look at Bannion and said something, but two more shots came from upstairs and Bannion, rushing headlong toward the stairs, paid no heed to the people around him.

Near the landing Bannion slowed with caution, and as he did so, a bullet came out of nowhere to strike solidly over his head and to one side. Bannion dropped down, drew his handgun, and risked a peek ahead.

There was no one visible in the hallway. There was not a sign of his five deputized cowboys.

The door to the King brothers' room hung ajar and acrid gunsmoke eddied outward there.

There were a number of closed doors on each side of this hallway, perhaps six of them. Then the hallway made an abrupt right turn going southward, but it seemed to Bannion from the sounds of that unseen battle, that the participants were to his left—either in the King brothers' room or the rooms adjoining it to the left.

He sprinted as far as Judith's room, kicked open the door, and jumped sideways against the wall with his cocked gun swinging.

Judith was in bed, sitting stiffly forward with a frightened, apprehensive look on her face. She called Bannion by name, then a solitary loud shot came, and she sat there clutching the bed clothing with her lips parted, saying nothing more.

Bannion lowered his gun. She was safe and there was no one with her. He said: "Lock this door after me, girl, and don't let anyone in here."

"Sheriff! What is it? What's happened?"

Bannion's bitterness almost let him tell her, but he didn't. He only repeated his previous instructions, and slipped back out in to the hallway. He stood there until he heard the lock click behind him, then he started forward very cautiously.

He was approaching the door that was ajar when a man rushed out of the room, saw Bannion, and jumped back. Evidently though, in that fleeting second, this man had recognized the sheriff because he called out, poked his head through the opening, and then stepped out fully.

It was one of the deputized cowboys. His face was white; his eyes were shades darker than usual.

"Damn!" he exclaimed to Bannion. "I thought you was another of 'em."

"Who?" demanded Bannion. "Where are they?"

"In the room beyond this here one. We was all sittin' out here, half asleep, when all of a damned sudden they opened up. They got one of the Kings . . . that dark feller whose eyes were swollen closed."

"Al?"

"Yeah . . . Al. They knocked him off his bed with the first shot."

"Killed him?"

"How the devil would I know?" exclaimed the agitated range man. "All hell busted loose. We smashed open the door, rushed in, and, Sheriff, the lead was flyin' thick as bumble bees. No one had time to look at that shot feller. All a man had time to do was drop down and try to get behind something." The rider started past. "I got to go," he stated. "I'm goin' downstairs and see if I can't find a way to come up behind them fellers. Hell, there must be ten of 'em in among these damn' rooms."

"There are three of them," stated Bannion, and

at the deputy's unbelieving look, he added: "Go on . . . tell the clerk downstairs to show you how to come up from the pantry. But, pardner, be awful careful. Those three men are professionals. They're some of the best gunfighters in Texas."

"That," snapped the cowboy, "is somethin' you sure didn't have to tell me, Sheriff."

Bannion watched his deputy hurry along to the stairs and go bouncing down them two at a time. He considered rushing after and joining him in his attempt to flank Hobart, Elam, and Fuller. But several loud shouts from the room where the Kings and his other men were battling it out changed his mind.

Bannion turned and moved slowly along the hallway until he was flattened to a wall outside the room. He waited there with good sense until he announced himself several times, then he whirled around the door casing and jumped inside.

Chapter Fifteen

Five guns had their smoking barrels trained unwaveringly upon Bannion.

Al King lay sprawled and unconscious beside his cot. One deputy was writhing upon the floor with a broken leg—the result of a bullet through his upper leg. Another deputy was attempting to staunch blood from a bad hole in his fleshy thigh. Ray and Hank and Austin King were flattened beside a shattered door leading into an adjoining room. Their faces were white and their eyes showed cruel lights. Two closely spaced gunshots erupted, echoing thunderously, from beyond the door and Bannion heard those bullets smack into the wall on either side of him.

Hank King shouted: "Down, Sheriff! Get away from the door!"

Bannion dropped, rolled sideways, and came up on his knees. He crawled to the first wounded deputy, wordlessly assisted this man at making his broken leg as comfortable as possible, then he went on to the second deputy. Here, though, that raw torn flesh had been staunched and the range man's white face looked dumbly at Bannion.

"No warning," this man gasped. "One shot through the window. Glass went showering all over. That dark one there beside his cot stopped that slug. Then hell busted loose. We run in . . . smack dab into the middle of it. That's when I stopped mine."

Bannion put a hand upon the cowboy's shoulder, gently squeezed, then turned as Ray King tapped him upon the back.

"I had no idea Rockland had gunfighters in his crew. They looked like ordinary ranch hands to me."

"Those men aren't part of Texas Star," Bannion told him. "They're professional killers. Hired gunfighters."

"But they're Rockland's, aren't they?"

Bannion nodded. "Yeah, they're Rockland's." He pointed over to Al. "How bad?"

"Through the lung. He's out and I hope he stays that way."

"I'll send for the doctor."

"You'll only get him killed, Bannion!" shouted Ray King over a fusillade. "The best thing for Al is to do exactly what he's doing right now . . . lie perfectly still and keep down."

Austin, along with Hank and Bannion's remaining two deputies, listened quietly as the gunfire dwindled, then they moved cautiously around the door and poured bullets into the adjoining room.

Bannion watched, waiting a moment before he asked Ray: "Where are they?"

"Scattered and out of sight. I think one is in the next room but we can't exactly poke our heads in there to find him. The others are in the room beyond the next one. They're somewhere along the walls on each side of that doorway. But they're no kids at this. After every shot they get quickly to some different spot. We've tried pattern-shooting until those walls look like sieves."

"And they're still shooting," said Bannion.

Ray King nodded. "Did they bother Judith?"

Bannion looked around. "No. Why should they, they work for her paw."

Ray inclined his head over this. He turned to look with narrowed eyes at the other defenders. He watched his brothers and those two cowboys fire and sidle away, return to fire again, and once more shift positions. He said: "Sheriff, this is getting to be a Mexican stand-off. They can't overwhelm us and we can't even find them. I sent one of your men downstairs to . . ."

"I know. I met him."

"Do you think it'll work?"

Bannion frowned. "The idea's sound enough, only those gunmen aren't tied to any trees. They can keep shifting, too. I'd have sent two men at the minimum."

"Couldn't spare 'em," Ray explained, and pointed toward his downed brother and the two disengaged deputies. "Those gunmen out there are damn' good. If the odds were even, I believe they'd try rushing us."

There came a lull now. While this uneasy silence lasted the men around Bannion looked from one to the other. Ray twisted to go back by the door but Bannion reached out his arm to detain him.

"I don't want those men to get away," he told Ray King. "I'm going to find that man you sent to flank them and join him."

Ray nodded at this.

Bannion managed to make it out of the room, down the hall to the stairs, and then down the steps without incident. He knew this building as well as its owners. He pushed on across the lobby, which was now empty, cut through the dining room, and entered the pantry. Here, he found the kitchen help huddled together. When they began asking questions, Bannion just shook his head at the lot of them and moved along to the rear stairway. Here, he paused to cock his head and listen.

Gunfire was rising to another crescendo overhead; the walls reverberated with each concussion. Bannion went cautiously up the stairs, and where the second floor showed, he halted to run a probing look in all directions. On his left and right were identical dark doors, both closed. Somewhere, up here, he would find his deputy. He did not move for a long time. Under circumstances like these, many men had been killed by friends. Bannion did not propose to have this happen to him, and yet he had no way of knowing where his deputy was.

It was impossible, except in a very general way, to determine where those exploding blasts were coming from. In this hotel nearly all the rooms had interconnecting doors, in case guests wished to engage more than one room.

Bannion went over the floor plan in his mind and decided that since the room where the Kings were was down the hall near its turning on the right-hand side, John Rockland's gunmen would have to be on that same side of the building. He passed swiftly up the remaining steps, paused for a second to take one final look around, then he went to the nearest door, opened it an inch, drew no fire, opened it wider, and looked in.

He was staring into a cocked gun ten feet across the room near a massive old dresser. There was neither time to draw and shoot or duck back. The man holding that gun straightened up.

It was Bannion's deputy, and the cowboy put a sardonic look upon Sheriff Bannion and dolefully wagged his head. It had, he was telling Bannion in this manner, been a very close call for the lawman.

Bannion gestured toward the splintered doorway between them. The cowboy inclined his head. Bannion took this to mean it was safe to enter, and did so, flattening at once along the wall and mincing his way forward to one side of the opened door. Across from him the deputy followed his example. When they were close, one on each side of the opening, they traded a long glance. A shot exploded inside, deafeningly close. Bannion gestured for the deputy to cover him. He dropped down flat on his stomach, flung off his hat, and pushed his head along the baseboard until, just short of being able to see around the door, he paused to look up. The deputy was raising his gun hand. Bannion took a shallow breath and stretched his neck.

He could see the entire east wall of the yonder room, and part of the north and south walls. There was no gunman in his sight. He drew back very carefully, pulled himself upright, yanked his hat back on, and gestured for the cowboy to step back away from his side of the door. This accomplished, Bannion balanced forward, set one foot as far forward as he dared, and whipped across that lethal opening in a swift blur of movement. Then he dropped down swiftly, waiting. Apparently he had not been seen, for no shots came.

He lay flat again, began to repeat his earlier maneuver, and a second before he pushed his head out, a slashing burst of searching gunfire erupted far ahead. Bullets struck the door making it quiver wildly. Bannion drew back and waited, thinking the King boys were proving an easy match for the men seeking to kill them.

When that unseen gunfighter opened up, returning the Kings' fire, Bannion shoved his head along the baseboard, straining to see the east and south walls. He saw them both in a flash; he also saw that gunfighter. He was down on one knee with his gun cocked and ready to fire through the other door into and out of that yonder room, which was positioned in the northern wall.

Bannion whipped forward his six-gun, steadied it, and fired. Something, perhaps Bannion's quick movement, alerted the gunfighter a fraction of a second ahead of Bannion's shot. The man was uncoiling up off the floor when Bannion's slug struck him. He got off a return shot with unbelievable speed, but then he went over sideways, rolling from the impact, came to rest hard against the east wall, and stayed there.

Bannion drew back. He put up a hand where his hat had been. Then slowly pulled his legs up and stood. The deputy was retrieving Bannion's hat and studying it. He put two fingers through the holes, one in the front and one in the back. He looked incredulously at Bannion while handing over the hat.

"Lord A'mighty," he mumbled. "That was the damnedest piece of shootin' I ever saw in my life. He was goin' down from your slug when he whirled around an' got off that shot."

Bannion examined his hat. Two inches lower and he would have been dead with a bullet lodged in his brain. For a moment it shook the sheriff, but then he put the hat back on, and shook off the feeling of relief. Gunfire erupted again and the cowboy had his mouth close to Bannion's ear.

"Dast we go in there . . . we might get up to that other door and get them other two."

Bannion considered this. He had no fears about passing undetected into the next room. All they would have to do in order to achieve this end would be to wait until the two gunmen were again engaged with the Kings, their attention fixed forward. What troubled him was that, once in the other room, they would be in more jeopardy than ever because, while they might catch the gun-fighters between their fire and the shooting of the Kings, they themselves would also be under fire from both sides.

The cowboy, though, was impatient. He began edging around Bannion. He had reloaded his handgun. He seemed almost eager now. Bannion looked closely at him. This man was young, per-haps no more than twenty-one or -two years of age. Bannion sighed, remembering how youth was a reckless time. He put out a hand, stopping the deputy, and moved ahead of him. If he was going to be shot, Bannion wanted to walk into it fully aware that he had taken all precautions. He had no relish for following some hot-headed youth into a lead storm.

Bannion got as close to the door as he dared. Then he waited. The firing in the rooms ahead had its high moments and its low moments. Bannion wanted to make his move during a high moment. This might increase the chances of an accidental strike, but he preferred this to being the target of the unerring aim of two men who were probably every bit as accurate and merciless as the man he had shot. Behind him, the deputy stirred restlessly, brushing up against Bannion.

Someone let out a fierce curse. Instantly the two gunmen opened up. This was precisely what Bannion had been waiting for. He struck backward with one hand to alert the deputy, then he jumped into the next room, threw himself violently sideways, and went bounding ahead during that furious forward exchange of shots until he was across the room on the right-hand side of the door.

The deputy, following Bannion's example, had raced across to the left-hand side of the same door. Both of them hung there, pressing to the wall, breathing deeply and involuntarily flinching from the ripping sound of lead slugs tearing into the woodwork around them.

The angry voice began again, calling his attackers vile names. Each time the voice rang out, it brought forth a rush of gunfire from the gunfighters. Bannion wondered whether the man yelling had a strategic reason for doing so, and if so what it could be.

The deputy moved to get Bannion's attention. He looked excited and was gesturing to the wall on his far left. He made a thumping motion with his gun hand, indicating, Bannion thought, that he had placed one of the gunfighters by the sound of the man's back or shoulders striking the wall. The deputy stepped back from the door, brought up his cocked six-gun, and frowned in powerful concentration. Bannion watched as the deputy took his time in determining exactly where to aim so that when he fired the man in the next room would be struck by that penetrating bullet. The sheriff thought of stopping the cowboy, knowing that their position would be revealed, but then it was too late.

The gun was fired. A shout rose beyond the wall. Bannion watched as a smile emerged on the face of his deputy. The sheriff, knowing the killers now knew they had enemies behind them, shifted and pushed into the deputy just as a barrage of shots blasted through the wall. Wood splinters and wall dust flew, and a commode bowl and pitcher upon a far table disintegrated from a direct hit.

Bannion was down flat. And right next to him was the cowboy, who was no longer grinning. In fact, he looked badly shaken, as he pressed his body into the floor to make it as flat as possible.

Although the deputy's bullet might have winged

a gunman, from the savage firing that had them pinned down now, Bannion knew that it had neither killed the man nor injured him very seriously. It had, however, accomplished something—it had directed the anger of those two killers toward Bannion and his companion and away from the King brothers and Bannion's other deputies.

Chapter Sixteen

From the other side of the wall came a triumphant shout and the shooting became even more deafening. As he lay on the floor, Bannion wished idly that the two gunfighters would recognize the futility of their position and give up since they were both outnumbered and cut off. They did not.

They seemed to be taking turns shooting—one spraying lead while the other one reloaded. Unless this was what they were doing, Bannion could not account for the volume and ferocity of their fire. It wasn't long before it began to seem to him that the pauses between the shots were growing longer. He lay on the floor, trying to be certain of this, thinking that, if this were so, the gunmen were probably running low on ammunition.

It did not occur to Bannion, until he heard the sound of a spur striking wood, that the gunfighters were making ready to escape out the window and back down the fire escape. Then he did a reckless thing. He got to his feet and sprang across the door opening to the room's west side, and kept right on going. As Bannion passed out into the hallway, his puzzled deputy called out. But Bannion kept right on going—down the stairs, through the abandoned kitchen, and then the storeroom, until he emerged in the alley. At once a bullet came. It pierced Bannion's shirt, low along his ribs, and the lawman hit the dirt, rolled, snapped off a shot without any actual target, and waited. No other shot came, but an angry curse did.

"Damn you, Bannion . . . you trying to get killed!"

Bannion knew the voice, but he did not at once place its owner. For that reason he scuttled behind a wood shed and waited a moment before peering out. It was then that he realized it was Ray King. As he looked out, he saw there was no one on the fire escape.

Bannion drew back a ragged breath, figuring Ray King's shot had warned the upstairs gunmen that there was an ambush awaiting them down below. He felt like swearing. He had had it all worked out so nicely in his mind. As the two gunfighters appeared on the fire escape on the side of the building, exposed and helpless, Bannion would demand their surrender and they would either throw down their weapons or be killed.

He waited, listening to the intermittent shooting inside the hotel. It seemed to be moving farther along the floor, from room to room. Then there came a long lull, some muffled cries, then a resumption of gunfire downstairs. Bannion shifted his gun hand to cover the rear door through which he had hurtled himself only minutes before. He risked a shout to Ray King.

"Sounds like they're making for the back door and this alleyway! Remember, King, I'm over here, too."

Ray stepped out into clear view. He had a direct northerly view of the hotel's rear wall as far, and farther, than that back door. Bannion's position by the shed was slightly south and east of that door.

They waited. Sudden silence came and in some ways it seemed more deafening than the earlier gunfire had been. During this lull Bannion took the pulse of his town. It was breathlessly still, hushed. No sounds of people out and about. They were obviously uncertain about what was going on, but they had not the slightest doubt concerning their individual parts in it—they kept entirely away.

The door slammed open. Two men sprinted out into the alley and ran directly forward from the hotel's rear wall some hundred feet apart. They twisted once or twice to fire behind them. A number of wild shots came from the rearward doorway but these were not at all accurate. Those racing men, protected in great measure by darkness, also ran unevenly, making of themselves difficult targets.

Bannion saw muzzle blast from Ray King's gun. He flinched. That whip-sawed red flame looked as though it was aimed directly at him. Ray fired a second time. Bannion waited, letting the two men come even with the shed. Ahead of them was an old, patched wooden fence. Beyond this was the rear yard of a house. Bannion raised his gun, tracked the nearest of his enemies, and tightened his finger a fraction of a second after a bullet struck wood beside his head. Bannion's bullet sang overhead and the gunman dropped to his knees, apparently stung by splintered wood. He swore heartily. Both gunmen then hit that fence in a plunging run and rose up to drop down somewhere beyond it.

In the excitement Bannion swore at Ray King. He remained on his knees long enough to reload, then he got up, and began yelling at his men as they came out of the hotel to circle around the square. Then he strode over to Ray King, who was also walking out into plain sight.

"I told you to be careful . . . that I was over there," rasped the sheriff to Ray King. "You spoiled my one good shot."

Ray considered the lawman's angry countenance. "There was a lot of lead flying," he said. "But if that was my fault . . . I'm sorry."

Bannion turned toward the fence. "Come on," he growled. "And after this you stay right beside me."

The big Texan viewed Bannion calmly, then went along without making any comment. At the fence they paused to listen. Bannion had no doubt but that those fugitives were a long way from the fence by now, but he wanted to be sure. When he was, he holstered his gun, reached up, and heaved himself over the fence. It shook under this strain, and as Bannion landed in someone's geranium bed, Ray King came vaulting over to land beside him.

In front of the hotel men were slapping saddle leather, and within seconds both Bannion and Ray could hear the horses racing around the square northward.

"They won't get away," Ray declared. "They may go into hiding, but they won't get away."

These were also Bannion's thoughts, but he said nothing. They squatted there by the fence with darkness around them, considering the forward stretch of open yard. Bannion was not anxious to step out into this and be exposed.

Ray King said: "Cover me. I'll go around the house on the south side."

Bannion rose up when Ray did, saying: "I'll go around on the north. We'll meet around front. And this time don't shoot me."

Ray's teeth flashed in a spontaneous grin, then he was gone, running hard. Bannion watched him gain half the distance of that exposed yard, then he rushed forward. No shots came at either of them.

Bannion whipped in close to the quiet and dark house, followed the full distance of its northernmost wall, and poked his head around front where the wall ended. Big Ray King was standing there in full view. He seemed to be listening to the night. Bannion walked over to him and turned at the sound of approaching horsemen.

Without waiting to determine who they were, Ray King said: "Come on. Those are my brothers."

Bannion was puzzled as to how Ray knew, but when he walked out to the roadway, there were Austin and Hank King on two fine-looking saddle horses.

"You see 'em?" Hank asked.

Ray said that he had not and Bannion shook his head. Austin remained only long enough to hear his brother's reply, then he whirled without word or a nod and went plunging back the way he had come.

"Where are my deputies?" asked Bannion, watching Austin King fade away in the darkness.

"We split up at the livery barn," explained Hank. "We came around this way . . . they went southward to . . ."

An abrupt burst of gunfire drowned out Hank's answer. Bannion turned and began running toward the racket. Someone behind him, either Ray or Hank King, called out: "Around by the livery barn!"

Hank shot ahead in a hunched-over run, passing Bannion in a flash. He was going south. Long before Bannion or long-legged Ray King got to the roadway's nearest southerly intersection, Hank was out of sight, heading west, back toward the heart of Perdition Wells.

"I don't know how . . . they did it," gasped Bannion. "Getting around us like that, and back to the barn."

Ray was leading now. He cut around the corner and went along as far as the juncture with Perdition Wells' north-south main roadway. Here he waited for Bannion to catch up. When the sheriff stood next to him, he said: "I don't know, either, but it was a wise move. They need horses right now more'n they need anything else."

More gunfire erupted, and this time Bannion and Ray could see the red flashes. Two deputies were across from the livery barn, hunkered behind a public watering trough. Their adversaries were deep inside the barn. Bannion took this in with one glance and grabbed Ray's arm.

"Around back," he panted, and struck out across the roadway with Ray running at his side. They made it to the alleyway and slowed here to begin a cautious advance northward.

"They sure as hell won't try riding out the front way into those guns," stated Bannion.

When they were within a hundred feet of the barn's wide rear opening, they stopped. "Now hold your fire," the sheriff said. "Let them think they can make it out the back way."

They waited there in the darkness made even

more so by the dusky shadows cast outward and downward from the surrounding buildings. They checked their handguns, as they listened to the firing from around front. They could tell there were more than just two guns there now.

Bannion's breathing was rattled; he had not done so much running on foot in years. Even through the darkness he could see the larger, younger man's twinkling look upon him, and he wagged his head.

"Never did believe the good Lord meant for a man to move fast afoot. If He had, He'd have given him four legs like He did with horses."

King's large, even white teeth flashed before he turned to continue watching the barn's rear opening. The fierce gunfire around front was dwindling. Then it swelled up again. Perhaps the men had stopped to reload or maybe they had sighted movement deep in that Stygian barn.

Bannion, feeling hot, feeling excited, moved forward another twenty feet. Ray trailed him. Now they stood quite close to that great dark opening, guns up and ready. Another lull in the firing, in which the two were able to hear horses snorting in fright, and one of the gunmen saying: "You go on, Brady. I'll keep 'em out until you bust clear out back. Just don't forget to go see that damned Rockland feller, if I end up in jail, and have him spring me."

There was no response to this, but from within

the barn a horse's shod hoofs struck wood.

"Saddling up," Bannion murmured. "Get set."

The two inched forward another few feet, tension rising up in each of them.

Ray King stood thoughtfully. He eased off with his cocked gun, holstered it, and when Bannion rolled his brows together in a dark scowl over this, Ray put his head down to whisper: "You want him alive, don't you?"

Bannion nodded.

"Then I'll bulldog him when he comes out that door, and then it's your turn to be blessed careful if you have to shoot."

Bannion hesitated as he'd done over at the hotel, trying to come to a decision about this plan. But Ray was already carefully moving ahead, and flattening himself against the wall at the doorless opening, his head cocked to one side, listening.

Across the way several probing shots were fired into the barn. One of the gunfighters swore viciously.

Then a voice from inside said: "Hurry up, dammit. They're likely to rush in here any minute or even get around in the back alley."

A stronger, waspish voice came right back, saying: "I *am* hurrying. This damned horse is all buzzed up from the shooting."

Bannion saw Ray bend forward from the waist and carefully edge his face around to look into the barn. The sheriff held his breath, hoping the gunfighters were too occupied to notice Ray, but also thinking that if they happened to see him, they were good enough shots to blast even that faint, thin target. Suddenly Ray whipped back, flexed his arms, and bent both knees outward in preparation to making a powerful lunge. Bannion could scarcely breathe as he imagined the gunfighter in the barn mounting. He raised his six-gun.

Bannion heard one of the men curse a horse coarsely. He also heard the excited prancing of that animal and the creak of leather. He saw the onward blur of movement start past the opening. He did not see Ray begin his hurtling leap, but he saw the horse stagger and he heard a man's startled outcry, then the horse shied violently, dumping both his rider and Ray King into the alleyway. Dust spurted where the two struck. The terrified horse went careening down the alleyway past Bannion, head up and stirrups flapping.

Ray was fighting a man as powerful as himself. Bannion saw that at once, but he couldn't help him because from within the barn came a savage shout and a searching, low shot.

Bannion rushed forward, poked his gun around the doorway, and fired twice, low and sideways. He waited by the doorway until, over his shoulder, he saw Ray rolling with both big arms locked around his adversary, attempting to get clear of the opening. Bannion saw them clear of the opening, and so ran out to distance himself from the building, then sprinted across the opening of the barn. He got close to the two men struggling in the dirt, stirring up clouds of dust, and halted, his gun hand up and ready.

It was not easy in that combination of threshing movement and darkness to determine which man was Ray King and which was not. But after a time Bannion was able to distinguish a thatch of red hair. Ray King's hair was chestnut-colored. Bannion reached down, caught that red-headed man by the scruff of his neck, steadied him briefly, and arced downward with his pistol barrel. The gunfighter fell limply, face down, in the dirt, and Ray, still straining, collapsed upon the suddenly unresisting form.

Chapter Seventeen

Three running shapes came noisily up the alleyway. Even though Bannion figured they would all be allies in this fight, he dropped to his knee between Ray King and the on-coming silhouettes. One of the men saw the moon glint upon Bannion's handgun and called out a quick warning. Immediately the trio dissolved into the shadowy gloom.

All was quiet for several seconds, then two shots slammed deep into the barn from across the road, their echoes running on out into the night.

From out of the darkness of the alleyway, someone said: "Hey . . . is that you up there, Ray? It's me . . . Hank. Austin and a deputy are with me. Ray? Are you all right?"

Bannion answered, lowering his weapon as he did so. "He's all right. A little spent and dirty, but unhurt. It's Sheriff Bannion. Come out slowly. . . ."

Three men stepped forward, converging near the center of the alleyway. They stepped along and then halted a few feet from where Bannion now stood. He recognized Austin first, who was craning his neck to see behind the sheriff. Ray King had managed to stand up, and he was knocking dirt from his clothing.

Before anyone could say anything, the lone deputy across the road fired another shot into the barn. There was no answering gunfire from the gunfighter inside, just as there hadn't been earlier when Bannion had fired into the barn. He called out to the deputy: "Hold your fire! Hold up for a minute around front."

Bannion looked at Ray and motioned for him to side him as he slowly began edging back to the barn opening.

All was quiet in the barn, and Bannion called out: "Stranger, your friend didn't get far trying to bust out on a horse! And you know your other friend is lying over at the hotel. You might want to surrender now, because, if you don't, we'll be rushing in from both the front and the back. You'll likely never live through it."

The men in the alleyway exchanged looks as Bannion's words were met with silence. They all looked worn out, but uninjured, although one of the deputies must have been nicked by a bullet as he had a handkerchief wrapped around his upper left arm.

"All right," came a thick voice from within the barn. "All right, come on in. My gun's empty."

"Just so there'll be no misunderstanding," Bannion said sardonically, "throw it out into the center of the runway."

The men listened and heard the gun, or something, strike in the livery barn dirt. Bannion took a long breath, stepped in front of the doorway. Ray came up next to him, and they entered, slowly and cautiously. Behind them the others moved steadily forward, guns up and ready.

"Over here," said a fading voice.

Following the sound, Bannion crossed to a tie stall. He could barely see the outline of a man's hat there in the straw bedding. "Fetch a lamp," he called, then put up his gun and stepped into the stall, and kneeled down beside the gunfighter. "How bad you hurt?" he asked.

"Oh, I'll probably make it," was the quiet answer to this. "Hit somewhere . . . there ain't no sense of pain. For that matter, lawman, there ain't no sensation of feelin' at all."

Ray King crouched down beside Bannion. The others stood outside the stall, this being a narrow tie stall without room for more than two men at a time.

Bannion looked around, saying irritably: "Where the hell is that lantern?"

"Coming!" Hank called, rushing out of a harness room with a desk lamp held high and flooding the barn with shifting light. "Be right there, Sheriff."

Bannion watched as orange-red light fell upon the injured man's face, his chest, then his lower body. He heard Ray draw back a sharp breath beside him.

The gunfighter raised himself up enough to look down his body.

"Well, I'll be damned," he said, then looked at Ray and Sheriff Bannion. "It's the big one. I didn't think it was serious. I was crossin' the barn here, from one side to the other, when them fellers across the way there first rushed up. The damned slug knocked me down, but it didn't hurt. I just crawled in here . . ."

Bannion looked around, met the eyes of one of the cowboys, and said: "Better go get Doc."

One of the deputies headed toward the front roadway. In the silence the remaining men listened to his diminishing footfalls. There was nothing to say. Nothing to do. The bullet that had downed this gunfighter had hit him in the back, gone straight through right about at his navel, blown out a big hole.

The gunfighter looked down at his booted feet; he seemed to be straining. Perspiration stood out on his upper lip and his forehead. Then he slumped, saying: "Can't move 'em. Can't move my legs. Can't even move my toes." He looked at Bannion. There was a graying pallor coming to his cheeks, to his lips. "Who the hell wants to spend their life ridin' a wheelchair." He tried to smile, but it was more a grimace. "You know somethin', lawman . . . this is real easy. I never saw a man die this easy before. No hurt, no struggle."

Bannion said: "What's your name?"

"Brady Elam."

"What was the name of the feller who tried riding out of here?"

"Hodge . . . Hodge Fuller. You fellers kill him in the alleyway?"

"Just knocked him out," said Bannion. Then he asked: "Would you like a slug of whiskey, Brady?"

"Yeah, I'd like that."

Hank said softly—"I'll get it."—and went running from the barn.

The doctor entered the barn through the front. Brady didn't seem to be aware of the medical man's fierce denunciations as he stamped deeper into the barn.

Then Brady Elam just tipped his head against Bannion's leg, and died.

Ray King got up and moved aside for the doctor, who got down with a grunt and a sharp look of anger at Bannion. The doctor bent, squinted into that serene countenance, then straightened up.

"You don't need me," he said to Bannion. "You need the undertaker. He's deader'n a chilled mackerel."

Bannion pushed himself up. "Yeah," he said softly, and moved clear of the tie stall. He touched Ray's arm, saying: "Let's get Fuller . . . take him along to my office."

The men filed out the barn's rear doorway, leaving Brady Elam for the undertaker.

Outside, Austin King helped get the groggy gunfighter to his feet. He shook him, braced him at the waist, and, with Ray's help, started him along toward Bannion's office. The doctor went along beside Bannion, occasionally looking slantwise into the sheriff's face.

Near the jailhouse he started to say: "Doyle . . ."

Bannion indicated with his hand that he didn't want to talk. "Later, Doc. Whatever it is . . . later."

"But this is important. It'll surprise hell out of you."

"I said later. Right now I've got no stomach for more trouble . . . or surprises, either."

The medical man looked around, taking in the King brothers, the deputies, before turning back to Bannion. He shrugged. "All right. If that's how you want it," he said, and continued to walk along beside the sheriff. When the others halted, moving aside for Bannion to enter the jailhouse first, the old medical practitioner stood there watching Bannion push on inside . . . and then stop with his back to everyone.

The doctor stepped through the door and hurried up to Bannion, saying: "I tried to tell you, Doyle."

In one of Bannion's two little strap-steel cells sat John Rockland. He looked rumpled and weary. He stood as Bannion stared with a puzzled expression.

Bannion turned to address the old doctor. "You . . . ?" he began.

"Yes . . . me . . . well, not alone. I told you I had a notion to get up a posse of my own and bring Rockland in. He didn't put up much of a fight, came in pretty willingly."

Bannion remembered his conversation with the doctor, in which he had said that Rockland deserved a humbling. He'd forgotten about it over the course of this day. He glanced at John Rockland, standing with his hands around the cell bars, and then went over to his desk, threw down his hat, and gestured for Austin and Ray King to put the gunfighter they were supporting into the second cell.

"Lock him up," he said, opening a drawer and taking out the ring of keys that held those to the cells, which he tossed to Ray.

When this had been accomplished, Bannion said to Ray: "Take Doc over to the hotel and see about Al. Then, after Doc's done with what he needs to do, send someone back here with word on whether Al's going to make it or not. If he isn't . . . Rockland and every man-jack who works for him will be charged with murder." He waved a hand in dismissal. "Go on."

Looking very uncomfortable, the only other man in the office—one of the deputized cowboys—quickly followed Ray and the doctor out the door, and gently closed it. Bannion sat down. He kicked his chair around and exchanged another long, silent stare with John Rockland. When he spoke, his voice sounded as dry as wind rustling old cornhusks.

"Now tell me you didn't send for those three gunfighters, Mister Rockland. Go ahead . . . lie to me so I can tell you exactly what I think of you."

Rockland dropped his hands from the cell bars. "I sent for them, Sheriff. But that was before the Kings saved Judy's life."

"Why didn't you stop them?"

"I . . . would have. I didn't think they'd arrive in town before tomorrow at the very earliest. Frankly I was worn out, dead-tired. And I had every intention of riding in tomorrow, paying them off, and sending them on their way. I had no idea . . ."

"Rockland, you're a fool. An arrogant, overbearing fool. I guess there's really nothing the law can do to you for what happened in Perdition Wells tonight . . . but as long as I live I'll never forget what trouble you caused here. And I doubt that I'll be the only one who remembers."

"Sheriff, I'm ashamed . . . and I'm very sorry," Rockland said.

"Hell," grumbled Bannion, "I've got a cellar full of apologies from fools like you. It makes me sick listening to you." Bannion turned away, the legs of the chair scraping across the floor. He brought out his six-gun, stared at it, and tossed it on his desk. Then he bent to make a cigarette. He sat and smoked it, then leaned back in the chair and closed his eyes. When a half hour had passed, he rolled another cigarette, which he was lighting when Ray King came in through the front door.

He smiled at Bannion, and told him the doctor's report was favorable. "Al's got a perforated lung," he said, "but the damage is high up, and likely he'll be all right. He'll need some time here to recover . . . bed rest . . . but he should be OK."

Bannion nodded his head, pursed his lips just as the door opened. Ray stepped aside. Bannion's hand stopped halfway to his face as his eyes fell upon Judith Rockland entering the office, wrapped in a heavy coat. Her eyes met those of her father in the cell.

Bannion stood up, casting a dark glance at Ray King. "She shouldn't be here, Ray. Doc said . . ."

"It wasn't my idea," Ray responded, shrugging. "I tried to talk her out of it."

Judith walked deliberately toward the cell, her gaze never faltering from her father's face. She stood there a long time, studying his face, ignoring both Bannion and Ray King who were both growing increasingly uncomfortable.

Finally she said: "Why did you do it? Last night when you came to my room at the hotel, you told me you were grateful to the Kings for saving my life. You said you were going to talk . . ."

"Judy, honey, I didn't mean for this to happen," John Rockland tried to explain. "I swear that to you."

"But it *did* happen," she insisted. "You sent for those killers, didn't you?"

"Yes, but that was before I knew they'd saved you . . ."

Judith stopped listening, turned her back on her father. Then she walked over to Ray King. "I know words aren't enough," she said, looking steadily into his eyes. "But they're all I can give you right now. I'm ashamed for my father. I'm sorry for what's happened tonight from the bottom of my heart. I'll do anything I can to set this to rights, Mister King."

Ray smiled. He reached out his hand, saying nothing. Judith put her fingers into that hand. Then Ray said gravely: "All right, Judy. The first thing you can do to help square things is come back to the hotel with me. You know you shouldn't have left. You're not completely recovered yet."

He then took her hand and laced it under and over his arm, patting her fingers as they rested on his upper arm. "May I escort you back?" he asked.

Judith nodded and smiled. She did not look back at her father. As they were passing through the door, Ray said loud enough for Bannion and her father to hear: "And the second thing you can do is let me take you riding when you're well again."

She looked at him with that disconcertingly level glance of hers, and said: "Mister King, if you hadn't asked me that, I was going to ask you."

Bannion got up from his desk chair and went

over to the door and gave it a good kick, then he stood a moment, considering John Rockland. He walked to his desk, picked up the keys, and scuffed over to the cell, which he unlocked. Then he stepped back and called Rockland several names, using what would be considered choice fighting words.

Almost meekly, Rockland passed out of the cell. He stopped next to Bannion. "I had that coming," he admitted. "All right, Sheriff. You've left me no doubt about how you feel toward me. Now it's up to me to prove that a man can return to what he once was." He continued to stand there.

Bannion crossed over to his roadside door and flung it wide open. "Get out of here," he ordered. "I can't stand the sight of you."

He closed the door, listening to Rockland's retreating footsteps, then he returned to his desk, dropped down there, picked up his unfinished cigarette from the ashtray, lit it, and blew out a big cloud of bluish smoke. He rummaged in a drawer for a nearly empty bottle of whiskey, poured himself a powerful drink, and downed it, neat. When his eyes began to water, he laughed and said aloud: "I didn't know I had any tears left in me." He rubbed his eyes, thinking that no man could ever become so old, so hardened to life, that he could not feel anguish for the shortcomings of other men.

About the Author

Lauran Paine who, under his own name and various pseudonyms has written over a thousand books, was born in Duluth, Minnesota. His family moved to California when he was at a young age and his apprenticeship as a Western writer came about through the years he spent in the livestock trade, rodeos, and even motion pictures where he served as an extra because of his expert horsemanship in several films starring movie cowboy Johnny Mack Brown. In the late 1930s, Paine trapped wild horses in northern Arizona and even, for a time, worked as a professional farrier. Paine came to know the Old West through the eyes of many who had been born in the previous century, and he learned that Western life had been very different from the way it was portrayed on the screen. "I knew men who had killed other men," he later recalled. "But they were the exceptions. Prior to and during the Depression, people were just too busy eking out an existence to indulge in Saturday-night brawls." He served in the U.S. Navy in the Second World War and began writing for Western pulp magazines following his discharge. It is interesting to note that all of his earliest novels (written under his own name and the pseudonym Mark Carrel) were published in the British market and he soon had as strong a following in that country as in the United States. Paine's Western fiction is characterized by strong plots, authenticity, an apparently effortless ability to construct situation and character, and a preference for building his stories upon a solid foundation of historical fact. *Adobe Empire* (1956), one of his best novels, is a fictionalized account of the last twenty years in the life of trader William Bent and, in an off-trail way, has a melancholy, bittersweet texture that is not easily forgotten. In later novels like *The White Bird* (1997) and *Cache Cañon* (1998), he showed that the special magic and power of his stories and characters had only matured along with his basic themes of changing times, changing attitudes, learning from experience, respecting Nature, and the yearning for a simpler, more moderate way of life.

Center Point Large Print
600 Brooks Road / PO Box 1
Thorndike ME 04986-0001 USA

(207) 568-3717

US & Canada:
1 800 929-9108
www.centerpointlargeprint.com